> **"High school is the hardest thing we're ever going to have to get through."**

I guessed that Andie was really talking about her reputation. I wasn't sure what to say in response. Did she want me to ask her about it?

Or did she think I was still so new at Fairview that I didn't know what the other guys said about her?

I didn't think about what I was going to say or do next. I just let my impulses take over. Leaning forward, I took her chin gently in one hand and kissed her.

Her lips tasted sweetly of apple pie and vanilla ice cream. I moved in closer, sliding my hand from her chin to the back of her neck and sinking further into the kiss, pressing my lips against hers a little harder.

And then she pushed me away. . . .

Super Edition

Andy & Andie

MALLE VALLIK

BANTAM BOOKS
NEW YORK · TORONTO · LONDON · SYDNEY · AUCKLAND

RL: 6, AGES 012 AND UP

ANDY & ANDIE
A Bantam Book / January 2000

Cover photography by Michael Segal.

Produced by 17th Street Productions, Inc.
33 West 17th Street
New York, NY 10011.

ISBN: 0-553-49321-3

Visit us on the Web! www.randomhouse.com/teens

Published simultaneously in the United States and Canada

Bantam Books is an imprint of Random House Children's Books, a
division of Random House, Inc. BANTAM BOOKS and the rooster
colophon are registered trademarks of Random House, Inc. Bantam Books,
1540 Broadway, New York, New York 10036.

PRINTED IN THE UNITED STATES OF AMERICA

OPM   0 9 8 7 6 5 4 3 2 1

To Vanessa Kettunen

Andy's
Side

One

"LATER, NERD BOY. Hello, popularity!"

I muttered the words—my new mantra—at the reflection staring back at me from the rearview mirror of my beat-up old Ford. The guy in the mirror looked pretty cool—baggy button-fly jeans, black T-shirt, hightops.

Okay, so I couldn't see most of that in the rearview. But I'd spent enough time staring at myself in the full-length mirror on the back of the bathroom door that morning while I was getting dressed for my first day at Fairview High to know what I looked like, head to toe.

Straightening the ultracool sunglasses that had cost me three weeks' worth of snow-shoveling money, I opened the car door and got out, almost stepping right into an ice-crusted puddle of slush. Whoever had plowed the student parking lot after the last snowstorm had left huge, dirty mounds of snow piled everywhere. It was a warm day for late January in northern Ohio, and the piles were starting to melt, dribbling into grayish rivers meandering across the cracked asphalt.

Glancing around the lot, I saw at least a dozen kids hanging out. A bunch of guys and girls were leaning against a long, low-slung car. Several of them were smoking cigarettes, and all of them were dressed in black. Obviously the rebel crowd. Then there was a small group of giggling girls who all seemed to be poring over the same magazine. They looked like freshmen—too young to worry about. On the other side of the parking lot were some big guys wearing letter jackets in Fairview's crimson-and-white school colors. Now, *they* looked a lot more interesting.

The only other person who wasn't with a group of friends was a cute, slender girl with pale blond hair that was pulled back in a high, springy ponytail. She was bending down to lock the door of her car, which was even smaller and more rusted-out than mine. I leaned forward slightly, trying to get a better look. For some reason it seemed very important to see her face. . . .

I straightened up as soon as I realized what I was doing—namely, acting like a total nerd who didn't know better than to gawk at strange girls with his mouth hanging open. Not wanting the blond girl—or any of the other kids—to catch me staring, I turned to get my first good look at my new high school. *Okay, Parker,* I told myself as I checked out the boxy brick building. *Remember, this is your chance to start over. So don't blow it.*

I nodded, remembering the promise I'd made to myself two months ago, when my parents first told me we were moving. The vow that this time school was going to be different.

This time I was going to be popular.

I knew I *looked* cool—that part had been easy once I'd put my mind to it. It was *acting* cool that was going to be tough. I mean, in one sense starting over at a whole new school, in a whole new state, would make things a little easier. Nobody in Fairview, Ohio, knew me. I could be whoever I wanted to be.

I just wished I didn't have to walk into my new school at the end of January, right in the middle of the year. And on a Thursday, no less.

"Andy," I muttered under my breath as I headed for the school's wide, glass-paned front doors. "Your name is Andy."

A passing teacher shot me a curious glance, probably wondering about the psycho new kid who was wandering along talking to himself. I felt my cheeks go red, and I quickly turned away.

Don't blow it! I told myself. *Use your brain, man. It's all mental.*

That made me feel a little more confident. I'd always been smart. That's not a brag, it's just the truth. If there was one thing you could say about Andrew Jackson Parker, it was that he had brains to spare. Actually, that's the only thing most of the people at my old school back in Chicago would've had to say about me.

But all that was going to change at Fairview High. Here I planned to try out for the baseball team, not the chess club. If someone pointed me in the direction of the computer lab, I would run in the opposite direction. And if someone mentioned *Star Trek,* I would pretend I'd never seen it, let alone dressed up as Mr. Spock for Halloween when I was a freshman.

My new look was the first step toward the new me. Like I said, that part was easy—new wardrobe, contact lenses, new haircut. Mom and Dad had been a little confused by all that, but luckily they'd been too busy with the move to ask too many questions about all the credit card bills.

Now it was time for the next step. New friends. Cool friends. Like those jocks in the parking lot. Maybe even a cute girlfriend, like the girl with the ponytail. In my old life, any girl who looked like her would have been way out of my league. I'd learned that the hard way. But now, who knew?

A blast of warm air hit me as I opened the school door. I looked around the big, square lobby, and the smell hit me. That universal school smell— a mix of chalk, sweat, cleaning products, and bad cafeteria food. It smelled just like my old school back in Chicago, and suddenly a wave of intense homesickness washed over me.

What was I doing here? I should be back home, where I knew where I belonged, not in this new, strange place, where anything could happen. For a second, I was so nervous that I almost turned around and walked right back out of Fairview High, new hightops and all.

Nothing ventured, nothing gained. I could almost hear my dad's voice saying his favorite phrase. For once, I sort of understood what he meant by it. Once my momentary freak-out passed, I remembered my plan. Yes, things were going to be different here. Different, and definitely better.

I put my hand into my jeans pocket, checking to make sure that my schedule and the letter from the school were still there. According to the letter, I was supposed to go to the school office first thing and check in with Mr. Wainscott, the school's vice principal. Only one problem remained: I had no idea where the office was.

I wandered through the lobby into a long, windowless hall lined with lockers. I turned slowly in a circle, trying to figure out which direction to go in.

"You look lost."

I turned and saw a tall, amazing-looking girl leaning against the row of lockers nearby, watching me. "Uh, what?" I mumbled, not sure if she was talking to me or not. I mean, back in Chicago, girls who looked like this never talked to me. They usually didn't even notice I existed.

She tossed her long, shiny dark brown hair over her shoulder and laughed. "Don't tell me," she said in a teasing voice. "You're not only lost,

5

you're a new exchange student from, like, Lithuania or someplace and you don't speak English."

I realized I was staring at her belly button, which was exposed—along with several inches of smooth, pale skin—by her formfitting cropped top. Dragging my eyes back to her face, I gulped. "Er, no," I said, trying to focus. Cool. I had to be cool. "I mean, I'm not from Lithuania. I'm from Chicago."

"Chicago." She raised one eyebrow, looking sort of impressed. "Wow. Fairview must seem like the land of the hicks to you."

I shrugged. "Oh, I don't know," I said as smoothly as I could manage. I gave her a long, lingering look, just like I'd practiced a million times in my mirror at home. "*Some* stuff here seems pretty cool."

It worked! She actually blushed a little, then tossed her hair again. "I'm Lauren, by the way," she said.

"Andr—er, Andy," I said. "Andy Parker." I almost stuck out my hand to shake, but I stopped myself just in time, shoving both hands into my pockets instead. "It's nice to meet you, Lauren. Really nice."

She smiled, looking pleased. "Come on, I'll take you to the office. That's where you need to go, right?" .

I'd pretty much forgotten about signing in by then. I was totally blown away by the fact that a girl—a gorgeous girl—was flirting with me. Me. Andrew Jackson Parker.

But that wasn't really true. Lauren wasn't flirting with Andrew Jackson Parker the nerd. She was flirting with Andy Parker, cool guy. I nodded at her, slipping back into my new role. "Thanks. That would be great."

We headed down the hall together. "So, what would make someone move from Chicago to Fairview, anyway?" Lauren asked, giving me a sidelong glance.

"My mom's job," I replied. "She got an offer to be head of the math department at the university here." I shrugged. "And my dad's a behavioral scientist, so he can work anywhere."

"Really." Lauren shot me a cautious look. "It sounds like your parents are real brains. Are you into that stuff too? You know, math and, like, behavior or whatever?"

Mayday! Mayday! I thought desperately.

"Nah," I said aloud, giving what I hoped was a casual shrug. "Their jobs are totally lame, if you ask me. I'm more into sports and, like, just hanging out, you know?"

I felt a little bad about putting down my parents' jobs. Actually, I think what they do is pretty amazing. But the math-and-science thing definitely wasn't working in my favor with Lauren.

She was smiling again now. "Yeah, I know what you mean," she agreed as we turned a corner and walked down another long hall. Most of the kids we passed waved to Lauren or said hello, and most of them also looked at me curiously. "My parents are both lawyers, and they think I should be one too. As if!" She made a gagging face. "They totally don't understand that I want to be an actress."

"Really? An actress? That's cool."

She chatted about her role in some upcoming school play for the next minute or two. I did my best to pay attention, but I was having a little trouble focusing. I was too amazed with how easy this was so far.

All too soon, Lauren stopped in front of a large, glassed-in reception area. She gestured at the door. "Here we are," she said. "Who are you supposed to see?"

I pulled the papers out of my pocket and pretended to read them, not wanting her to guess that I'd memorized my schedule and the names of all my teachers. Some of the old Andrew-the-brain qualities were harder to change than others. "Uh, some guy named Wainscott . . ."

She wrinkled her nose. "Wainscott's the vice principal. He's, like, the patron saint of nerds or something. I mean, he thinks everybody should be totally interested in homework and academics and stuff. He's also the sponsor for the debate team here, so I should warn you he'll probably try to rope you into joining. He does that when anyone new starts, especially if he thinks they might be a brain."

For a second I felt excited. *A debate team?* I thought eagerly. *I didn't even know they had one here!*

Then, suddenly, I remembered. Cool guys didn't get worked up about nerdy stuff like that. Cool guys joined the baseball team, not the debate team.

Luckily, Lauren didn't seem to notice my momentary lapse into Andrew-ness. "See you later," she said with a little wave.

"See you around," I said, hoping it was true. I definitely wanted to see more of Lauren—and all of her cool friends. Maybe she even knew that girl with the ponytail. . . .

I opened the door to the school office and walked inside. A few minutes later I was shaking hands with a short, portly man with a fringe of brownish gray hair circling an otherwise bald head. Mr. Wainscott.

"Mr. Parker!" he exclaimed, finally dropping my hand and rubbing his own together eagerly. "Welcome to Fairview High. It's marvelous to meet you. The principal at your old school called me personally to tell me what a fine young man you are."

Uh-oh, I thought, my heart sinking. *Maybe I'm not making a totally fresh start here after all.*

Mr. Wainscott settled back on his chair and flipped through some papers. My academic record. Despite the laws of science, I wished it could spontaneously combust. What if Mr. Wainscott told

everyone I was really a nerd? I could see it now—
he would call a school assembly to introduce me.
*Please welcome Andrew Jackson "Geekazoid"
Parker,* he would say proudly. *He loves chess more
than life itself, and he can convert miles into kilo-
meters in his head. Among his other talents are
building shortwave radios, astronomy, and wiping
his glasses on his sleeve. . . .*

I snapped out of it and realized that Mr.
Wainscott was talking as he pored over my record.
"I see here that you participated in a lot of clubs and
other activities at your old school," he said. "I do
hope you'll get involved in things here as well. Our
debate team is one of the best in the region. Plus
the chess club has been low on membership, and I
see here that you won the state championship."

"That was last year, sir," I managed to squeeze
out from my tight throat. Why hadn't I hacked
into the school records and changed my paper-
work? Illegal or not, it would have saved me a
whole lot of potential humiliation. "I don't play
chess anymore."

Mr. Wainscott looked up from my record and
blinked at me, looking puzzled. "You don't? But
your old principal said—"

"I had a bad game. Uh, I mean a traumatic experience. Yeah, that was it," I hurried on, even
though I realized my story was more than a little
lame. "I went crazy after my last game—couldn't
eat or sleep or even study. The doctors said it was
stress, and they recommended I shouldn't play

10

anymore." I shrugged and smiled weakly. "So I think here at Fairview I'll probably just focus on sports instead."

"Sports." Mr. Wainscott ran a hand over his shiny head, looking completely confused. "Er, I see."

"Sports," I repeated brightly. "Specifically baseball."

As the vice principal cast a doubtful look from my record to me again, looking me up and down, I suddenly became aware of how I was sitting. I was leaning forward in my chair, my back straight and my hands folded in my lap like a good little nerd.

Yow, I thought. *Gotta remember that body language.* I thought back to how the cool kids in my last school always sat. I slouched down in my chair, trying to look as bored as possible. Kicking out my legs, I almost knocked over a potted plant with one of my hightops.

Mr. Wainscott didn't notice. He was staring at my records blankly. I could just imagine what he was thinking. He was trying to square the cool-looking, sharply dressed dude slouching in the chair across the desk from him with the dweeby teacher's pet I looked like on paper. I mean, not only were my grades a long, practically unbroken line of A's and A-pluses since kindergarten, but then there were the activities—captain of the chess club, leader of the Junior Astronauts, audiovisual aide, volunteer math tutor, and enthusiastic participant in the after-school Japanese classes.

Ugh, I thought as I mentally scanned my school career. *How did I manage to avoid seeing what a dweeb I was before? If it hadn't been for Amber—*

I stopped that line of thought right there. I definitely didn't want to think about Amber right then. Or ever again, if possible.

"Well, if you'd rather not play chess, that's fine," Mr. Wainscott said. "But how about joining the debate team? That might be a nice change of pace."

I almost laughed, remembering Lauren's warning. "I'm sorry," I said, keeping a straight face, "but I really don't think that's a good idea. Uh, I'd really rather concentrate on my schoolwork for a while."

That made him smile approvingly. "Very well," he agreed. "What are your plans after you finish high school? Are you planning to follow in your parents' footsteps and go into the sciences?"

"Uh, I'm really not sure." I planned to worry about my future later. First I needed to get my present under control. "I guess I haven't decided yet."

Mr. Wainscott nodded. "Well, you still have a few months before you'll have to start thinking about those college applications." He closed my file, then shuffled through the papers on his desk, frowning at two of them before he found what he was looking for. "Here's a copy of your class schedule. I hope you'll think some more about the debate team once you've settled in. But either way, we're happy to have a fine student like you on board, Andrew."

"Andy," I corrected quickly. Andrew was dead. Long live Andy.

Mr. Wainscott stood and walked to his office door, gesturing for me to follow. "I've asked a student who shares your schedule to show you around," he said. "Come along, he should be waiting."

I followed him out of his office into the reception area. There was a row of chairs facing the school secretary's desk, and two of them were occupied. I gulped, wondering which of the guys sitting there was supposed to be my guide.

The first guy was reading a textbook and frowning in concentration. He wore a plaid shirt made out of some cheap polyester blend and wrinkled khakis that were belted tightly around a too-skinny frame. His skin was pale and splotched with acne, his brown hair stuck up in random clumps, and his glasses were too big for his face, giving him the look of a confused bug.

The other guy had close-cropped sandy hair and a handsome, ruddy face. His rugby shirt stretched tightly across broad, muscular shoulders, and he was wearing hightops just like mine, except that they were probably three or four sizes larger. His arms were crossed over his chest and both legs were stretched out in front of him. He looked as though he was sleeping.

Jock. Definitely a jock.

Mr. Wainscott cleared his throat loudly, and the jock yawned and opened his eyes. If he noticed either myself or Insect Boy, who had finally glanced up from his book, he didn't indicate it as he stood and stretched.

Mr. Wainscott couldn't suppress his irritation. "Mr. Wilkins, you had the entire weekend to sleep."

"Too much to do, Mr. W. I've got a busy life, you know. So I figured this is as good a time as any to catch a few Z's." He looked at me and nodded but didn't say anything. Was his jock alert system for nerds working overtime? I could imagine a little bell ringing away in his head as the Nerd-O-Meter reached maximum load. Then he turned back to the vice principal, reaching into his pocket. "I've got this detention note you've gotta sign."

Rolling his eyes, the vice principal took the note, scanned it, and signed it. "There you are, Jake. Now get to homeroom. Pronto."

My heart sank as I realized what his words meant. Sure enough, Mr. Wainscott turned to the skinny dweeb with a smile. "Wendell, this is the new student I told you about. Andrew Parker, meet Wendell Owen."

Wendell stood and offered his hand, and I felt sick to my stomach. *No!* I wanted to scream. *I'm not like this anymore! I'm not a Wendell Owen.* But all I could say was, "It's Andy. Not Andrew, Andy," as I shook his hand.

Wendell beamed at me, pumping my hand up

and down. His palm was sweaty, and I thought I caught a whiff of onion on his breath.

I couldn't bring myself to look over at Jake Wilkins, but I could imagine what he was thinking: *Two of a kind. Twin losers.* Maybe Wendell and I didn't look anything alike anymore. But it was really starting to seem that despite all my efforts, I was going to be filed right back where I belonged—under *L* for *loser*.

Mr. Wainscott was rubbing his hands together as he watched us. "Wendell, my boy," he said, "if you could show Parker around, I'd appreciate it. I think you two have a lot in common."

Jake snorted loudly. Mr. Wainscott and Wendell ignored the sound, but I glanced over at him with surprise. Jake rolled his eyes and jerked one beefy thumb at Wendell, making the *L*-for-*loser* sign on his forehead with his other thumb and forefinger.

I couldn't believe it. Tentatively I smiled at him and shrugged slightly. Jake grinned and waved as he turned and headed out of the office.

Wow, I thought, staring after him, hardly hearing Wendell gushing about how well equipped the science labs were at Fairview, or something like that. *Did that really just happen?*

I was in kind of a daze as I followed Wendell out of the office. He led me to my locker and showed me how to work the combination lock. Then he pulled a sheet of paper out of the back of his textbook. "Mr. Wainscott gave me your schedule last week, so I came up with a schematic diagram on my computer over the weekend showing you the shortest route from class to class."

For a second I was impressed. I'd never thought of doing that, and my mind automatically started working out the process I could have used as well as the time it might have saved me at my old school.

Then I stopped myself, feeling panicky. I had to break my geeky habits—the mental ones, not only the physical ones. I tried to imagine how someone like Jake Wilkins might respond to what Wendell had done. "Hey, whatever," I said in a bored voice. "I'm really not that interested in getting to class quickly, you know?" I slouched against the lockers.

Wendell looked confused. He pushed his glasses up on his nose, and I had to refrain from doing the same myself out of force of habit. Even though I'd been wearing my new contacts for several weeks now, I still occasionally caught myself reaching up to adjust the Coke-bottle glasses that were no longer there.

"I also marked where the jocks usually hang out every hour," Wendell went on after a second, tapping the paper with his finger. "I use the schedule to avoid them."

"You've marked out where the cool guys are every hour?" Suddenly a lot more interested in his schematic diagram, I grabbed the paper out of his hand. "Let me see."

He smiled nervously, looking startled. "Sure."

I felt bad for a second. Wendell was trying to be nice, and I was being kind of rude. To distract myself from the guilt, I scanned Wendell's diagram. That did the trick. It was perfect. Wendell had even included names—Kyle Bladen. Fuzzy Rywinski. And, of course, right at the top of the list was Jake Wilkins.

"Thanks, Wendell." I slapped him on the shoulder. "I owe you." I started to move away from him, eager to start scoping out the jock hangouts and figuring out my best plan of attack.

Wendell grabbed my sleeve. "Wait! I thought I could show you around," he said, his face and voice pathetically eager.

I could imagine how he felt. After hearing about me from Mr. Wainscott, he'd probably thought I was a shoo-in to be his new best friend. And it was true that back at my old school, Wendell and I probably would have been the best of buds.

But not anymore. I couldn't afford to give Wendell the wrong idea. He wasn't the kind of friend I was looking for here. I couldn't start hanging out with him. Not even for a little while. Not even out of pity. That would be a one-way ticket straight to Loserville.

"Sorry," I told him. "I like to check out the action myself. Thanks for this, though. It's going to be a big help." I walked away from him, pretending not to notice how disappointed he looked.

After all, I had my own life to worry about.

TWO

DURING MY FIRST two classes I didn't have much of a chance to talk to anybody. In first-period English I was so careful to avoid sitting near Wendell that I ended up in a corner with nobody on either side of me. Then in music appreciation the teacher seated us in alphabetical order. I ended up at the end of a row, between a sullen girl with black lipstick and a dragon tattoo and yet another empty chair.

I vowed to do better in third period, psychology.

The classroom was in the science wing, which was at the other end of the school from the music room. By the time I got there, most of the class seemed to be seated already.

I paused in the doorway, a little breathless from the long jog across the school. Instead of normal desks and chairs, the room had a dozen lab tables set up facing a larger table in front of the wall-sized

18

chalkboard. The students perched on high wooden stools. One of the side walls was taken up by windows overlooking the faculty parking lot. The back wall was covered with diagrams of the human brain and a few other scientific charts and posters.

Seeing Wendell sitting by himself at a table in the front row, I had a brief urge to go and sit with him. After all, if it hadn't been for his diagram, I probably would have been late to every class so far.

Then he turned and saw me. His spotty bug-eyed face broke into a grin, and he waved. I mean, really *waved*. As in sticking his whole arm up in the air and thrashing it back and forth like he was bringing in a 747 at O'Hare Airport. His right hand almost smacked into a stylishly dressed auburn-haired girl who was sitting at the table behind him. She ducked just in time, then rolled her eyes and said something to the petite, curvaceous blonde beside her. The second girl giggled, and both of them turned to gaze at me curiously.

I winced and turned away, pretending I hadn't noticed either the two gorgeous girls staring at me or Wendell, who was still waving enthusiastically. I had just seen my future at this school if I decided to sit with Wendell.

That was when I spotted Jake Wilkins sitting at a table across the aisle from the two gorgeous girls. He was leaning back on his high wooden stool, balancing expertly as he talked to the two guys sharing the table behind him. One of them was tall and angular, with sharp features and really cool dreadlocks. The other was even bigger and beefier than Jake. His blond hair was buzzed almost to the skin, making his large, round head look a little like an overripe peach.

This was it. This was my big chance.

My heart hammering in my chest, I strolled down the aisle, trying to look casual. I stopped beside Jake's table.

"Hey," I said. "Seat taken?"

Jake glanced up and saw me. I was half expecting him to frown and say, *Take a hike, nerd.* Maybe shove me into the girls across the aisle just to make his point.

Instead he smiled at me. "Yo," he said. "The new kid. Plant it, dude."

I decided to take that as a yes, and slid onto the empty stool beside Jake. "Thanks."

"No big. So what's up? Oh, yeah, I'm Jake, by the way."

I know. I almost said it but stopped myself in time. "Hey," I responded instead, trying to sound bored and friendly at the same time. "I'm Andy. Andy Parker. I just moved here from Chicago."

"Really? I'm sorry." Jake laughed at his own joke. The two guys sitting behind us chuckled too. "Oh, hey, Parker," Jake said, swiveling again to point to the angular black guy. "This here's my main man, Bladen. Kyle Bladen. You know, sort of like 'Bond, James Bond.' And this . . ." He gestured to Peach-head. "This here's Mr. Rywinski.

His mommy calls him Robert James. But everyone else just calls him Fuzzy."

I grinned. Fuzzy. Perfect. "Hey," I greeted both guys, adding the requisite nod.

"Yo," Fuzzy replied. "How's it going, Parker?" He leaned forward to punch Jake on the shoulder.

Kyle said hi to me too. "So how's your first day going?"

"Okay so far, I guess," I said with a casual shrug. I nodded at Kyle's letter jacket, which was draped over the desk in front of him. "What do you play?"

"Basketball," Jake replied for him. "We both do. But Fuzzy's muscles get in the way. He can't run to save his life."

Fuzzy rolled his eyes at me. "See what I have to put up with?" he said, though he really didn't seem mad at his friend's teasing at all. "So, Parker, you into sports?"

"Sure," I said. "Uh, I was planning to try out for baseball in the spring. Is the team here any good?"

"Not bad," Kyle said. "We would've gone to regionals last year if we hadn't blown the Centennial game."

The three of them started discussing the previous year's season. I just sat and listened, a little stunned at what was happening. These three cool guys were treating me like one of their own!

I glanced forward, checking to see if the teacher had entered yet. Instead I saw Wendell

21

staring at me. His eyes were magnified by his thick glasses, which made their confused and slightly hurt expression all that much easier to read. I swallowed hard, flashing back to my old life. To all the times I'd sat there, feeling totally left out as the cooler guys talked about girls who treated me like I was invisible and parties I wasn't invited to. Totally ignoring me unless they needed tutoring for the next math test or someone to correct their latest English paper. Did I really want to be that kind of guy?

Then all thoughts of Wendell left my mind as another student rushed into class, clasping an armful of books to her chest. It was the girl with the ponytail—the one I'd noticed standing by herself in the parking lot.

I gulped as I finally got a good look at her face. She was beautiful. Strands of her hair, so pale blond that it almost looked white under the harsh fluorescents, floated around her pretty heart-shaped face. The only makeup she was wearing was a touch of pink gloss on her lips. That was all she needed. I realized I was staring at her, but I couldn't seem to stop. She was perfect. An angel.

The girl looked around, obviously searching for a seat. There were only two empty stools left in the room. One was at the table across from Kyle and Fuzzy. A stunning Asian girl with the longest legs I'd ever seen was sitting there, one slim elbow propped on the Formica tabletop as she twirled a strand of shiny dark hair around one finger. The two hot girls at the table in front of her had turned around to talk to her, and I guessed that they were all friends.

I expected the angel to head over and sit down with them. Instead, to my surprise, she scurried toward the empty seat beside Wendell.

Huh? I thought, wondering if my careful study of high-school society had some holes in it after all. I'd had no trouble scoping out the school's coolest jocks. And unless I missed my guess, the three girls across the aisle were part of the same popular crowd.

So what was up with this girl? She was just as pretty as the trio across the way—prettier, actually. Why would she sit with Wendell? It was like the queen of England suddenly deciding to have dinner at McDonald's.

I had to know what was going on. I waited for a pause in the guys' discussion of Jake's pitching style, then leaned in and interrupted. "Who's that?" I asked, trying to sound casual. I nodded toward Wendell's table. "The cute girl with the ponytail."

My three new friends traded a grin. After a meaningful pause, Jake finally answered. "That's Andie Foster. She's hot," he said. "Right, Fuzz?"

Fuzzy winked, his wide face arranging itself into a smirk. "You know it, man."

That didn't really answer my question. But at that moment the teacher strode into the room, putting a stop to the conversation.

I didn't really mind. There was plenty of time to find out more about the most beautiful girl in the school. For now, it was enough that I knew her name.

Andie Foster wasn't in any of my other classes that day except for calculus, and none of my new jock buddies were in that class, so I couldn't ask them about her. But I managed to forget about her—mostly—as I got to know some of the other kids in the cool crowd. Jake was in several of my classes, and he introduced me to all of his friends, including the three hot girls from across the aisle in psych class and Lauren Epps, the girl I'd met that morning.

But not Andie. None of them mentioned her at all. And I couldn't seem to come up with a nonchalant, cool way to bring up her name.

When I walked into psych the next day, panting from my run across the school, I was determined to find out more about her. But to my dismay, Ms. Church was already there. She started class before I could say more than "Hey" to the guys, and kept us too busy to talk.

At the end of class I forgot about Andie for the moment as I realized it was Friday—which meant that my first weekend as a Fairview High student began in just a few short hours. This was my chance to hang out with my new friends—that was how I was already starting to think of them— outside of school. I just hoped I didn't blow it and start talking about Klingons or something.

Working up my nerve, I turned to Jake, who was shoving his books into his crimson-and-white Fairview Warriors duffel bag. "So," I said offhandedly, "what do people in this town do for fun on the weekends?"

I figured that he didn't need to know what I used to do for fun back in Chicago. Somehow, whatever he might say in response to my question, I doubted that "helping my mother correct college-level math papers" or "playing virtual chess with my cousin in Florida" were going to rate high on the list.

Jake shrugged. "Normally there's not much to do around this lame town. We just hang out at Moe's Burgers, hit the movies, stupid stuff like that. But this weekend the Fuzzman and I are going to his older brother's wedding up in Michigan. And you know what that means." He turned and slapped hands with Fuzzy. "Older babes!"

"*Drunk* older babes," Fuzzy corrected with a leer.

"Oh. Sounds like fun." I was disappointed. So much for my big dreams of partying with the popular crowd that weekend.

I turned toward Kyle to ask what his plans were. But before I could open my mouth, Courtney Calhoun, the cute blonde from across the aisle, came over and wrapped her arms around Kyle's neck. "Hey, baby," she cooed into his ear before planting a kiss on his forehead, smoothing back his dreads. "I forgot to ask in homeroom—did you get tickets for that concert tonight?"

Kyle nodded, grabbing her elbow and pulling her down onto his lap. He gently pushed back a stray lock of her wavy blond hair. "What time should I pick you up?"

Jake rolled his eyes. "As you can see, Kyle's totally whipped," he said in a loud stage whisper.

"Shut up, man," Kyle shot back. "You're just jealous because no girl ever wants to go out with you more than once."

Courtney giggled. "Poor Jakie-poo," she crooned. "Unlucky in love."

"Yeah, right." Jake grinned and elbowed me in the ribs. "Poor Kyle is more like it. Courtney's really got you snowed, man. Don't you know that variety is the spice of life?"

I smiled weakly, trying not to wince at the blow to my ribs. Even after only a day and a half at Fairview High, I knew that Jake wasn't just blowing smoke. He'd already dated half of the cute girls in the junior class, along with a few seniors and a sophomore or two. During gym class, Fuzzy had noticed me watching Marissa Carpenter, the auburn-haired hottie from psych class, and told me all about her recent fling with Jake. According to him, the two of them had been hot and heavy for the better part of a month before breaking up a few weeks earlier.

As I watched Kyle and Courtney whisper to

each other, with his arms around her waist and her delicate hands buried in his thick hair, I couldn't help disagreeing. I really wasn't sure what Kyle saw in Courtney, other than her obvious physical attributes. She seemed like kind of an airhead to me. Still, the way the two of them were looking at each other made it clear that neither of them had any interest in anyone else.

Would a girl ever look at me that way? Unbidden, my gaze skittered toward Andie Foster's seat.

But she had already disappeared.

Three

"OH, MAN," JAKE groaned as he walked into psych class on Monday. "I can't believe I forgot. It's egg week!"

I glanced at Jake as I followed him into the room. I'd run into him in the hallway outside the classroom. He was talking to Veronica Morita, the Asian girl with the killer legs. From the way he was looking at her, I guessed that she was the latest spice he wanted to add to his life.

"What's egg week?" I asked as Jake and I took our seats in front of Fuzzy and Kyle.

"Egg week!" Fuzzy smacked himself on his broad forehead.

"I'll take mine scrambled," Kyle added with a grimace.

Jake rolled his eyes. "It's a lame marriage-and-responsibility project the whole junior class has to do every year."

"I wonder if we get to pick our own partners," Kyle mused, his gaze wandering across the aisle to Courtney, who was filing her nails as she talked to Marissa and Veronica.

Jake perked up a little at that. "I don't know," he said. "But now that you mention it, it could be fun to test-drive a wife for a while. The *right* wife." He glanced across the aisle and grinned. "You know, I was just thinking that Veronica and I would make a mighty fine couple at the Valentine's dance this year."

I just stared at him, perplexed by the sudden change of subject.

But Kyle laughed and leaned forward to punch him in the shoulder. "Yeah, right. Like she'd ever give you a second look after everything Marissa's probably told her about you."

"My point exactly." Jake grinned wickedly. "After being married to a great guy like me for a week, how could she resist? No matter what Marissa says."

Kyle turned to me. "Did anyone clue you in about the dance yet?" he asked. "It's, like, the social event of the winter. Almost as major as the prom." He shrugged. "Courtney says Lauren Epps thinks you're cute. Maybe you should ask her, eh, buddy?"

"She—She said that?" I could feel my face flushing and dropped my notebook so I could pretend the rush of blood to my face was from the change in altitude. I wasn't used to having girls discuss me with each other. Especially not amazing, popular girls like Courtney and Lauren. I didn't know what to think. And I certainly didn't know what to say, although Kyle seemed to expect some kind of response.

Luckily Ms. Church walked into class at that moment and saved me. "Good morning, kiddos," she greeted us as usual in her brisk, no-nonsense manner. "Welcome to married-with-children week."

She pushed her mass of dark, curly hair out of her face and leaned over to pull something out of her leather knapsack. When she held it up, I saw that it was a carton of eggs. Grade A jumbo.

"Some of you may have heard about this exercise from last year's group," the teacher went on, setting the carton on her desk and opening it. She picked out a smooth, white egg and held it up for us to see. "Each of these fragile, helpless eggs represents a baby. For the next week, you all are going to find out a little about what being parents is like."

Now I was starting to catch on. I'd seen this on an episode of *Buffy the Vampire Slayer*. Except of course in that case the eggs had hatched some kind of demon that took control of your mind and body.

I smiled at the thought. Compared to that, this project would be a breeze.

Ms. Church was still explaining. "You'll be expected to work as a team throughout this project, caring for your baby egg together. I've assigned all of you into couples, so forget about picking your own partners."

I heard Jake groan with disappointment. I smothered a laugh. So much for his big plans to woo Veronica.

The teacher held up a stack of papers. "I've also printed up a chart with steps for you to check off. For instance, I expect each couple to keep a journal detailing the assignments and what you learn about being a parent. One of you has to look after the egg at all times. Being good parents also means fitting in all sorts of things while still caring for your child. You'll be expected to create a budget, do household chores, cook a meal or two, and yes, even get along with your in-laws."

"A baby and in-laws in the same week?" Fuzzy groused. "You're killing me, Ms. Church. A guy can only take so much."

The class laughed, and even Ms. Church chuckled. "Welcome to the real world, Mr. Rywinski."

Courtney raised her hand. "My mom is always complaining about how much our maid charges us. If I do all this cooking and cleaning for this project, she'll probably expect me to, like, take over Rosa's job all the time." She actually sounded worried. Like, *sincerely* worried.

Ms. Church didn't bother to respond. "Oh, and I almost forgot," she said. "The husband and wife will also have to go on at least one date."

Jake and Kyle high-fived each other. "All right!" Jake crowed. "Finally, a teacher who assigns good homework! Ms. Church, you're awesome!"

Ms. Church laughed again. "Hold it, people," she warned. "This isn't all fun and games, you know. When you have to take care of a baby"—she held up the egg again—"making time for yourselves as a couple is very important. A baby can disrupt a relationship. You need to learn how to balance a lot of different things going on in your life. You may think being a teenager is tough, and it is, but being a parent is just as hard. And you're about to get a small taste of it."

Marissa raised her hand. "Ms. Church," she said, cracking her gum, "if we're doing all this stuff with the baby, and cooking and cleaning and stuff, well, when are we supposed to do our homework?"

Jake snorted. "Since when do you care about doing your homework, princess?"

Ms. Church glared at him, silencing him completely. Then she turned to Marissa. "Ms. Carpenter, you've raised a very good point. All of you are going to have a busy week looking after the egg *and* completing your regular schoolwork. Your boss isn't going to give you a day off if your baby is cranky, so neither will any of your teachers. Having a baby is an awesome responsibility—that's just something to think about. Especially at your age."

Veronica rolled her eyes and sighed. "We know that, Ms. Church," she called out in a lazy, bored voice. "Can't we just agree not to get pregnant and skip the assignment?"

Ms. Church smiled and shook her head. "Promises can be made a little too easily at your age, Ms. Morita, especially when your boyfriend promises to love you forever if only you'll go all the way."

The class tittered nervously at her blunt words, me included. In my old school, none of the teachers ever talked to us straight up like that. I decided I liked Ms. Church.

"Okay, listen up, kiddos." Ms. Church put on her glasses and picked up a piece of paper from her desk. "I have your partners."

There were whispers and stifled laughter from all over the room. But I sat very still, feeling tense. Glancing around the room, I wondered whom I would end up with. With my luck, there would be more guys than girls and I'd get stuck being partners with Wendell.

I shuddered at the thought. But a quick head count reassured me—the numbers were exactly even. Whew!

Ms. Church had assigned a couple of pairings already, handing out eggs as she went. Then she nodded at Veronica. "Ms. Morita," she said. She glanced at her list. "You'll be working with Mr. Wilkins."

"All right!" Jake whooped, making the whole class laugh.

I glanced over at the girls' tables. Veronica was rolling her eyes, pretending to be disgusted as she accepted the egg Ms. Church handed her, but I could tell she was flattered that Jake was so excited. At the table ahead of her, though, Marissa was frowning.

"My condolences, V," Marissa told Veronica loudly, leaning back and patting her on the arm. "But don't worry. My dad's a divorce lawyer, remember?"

Everyone laughed even harder at that. "Enough, Ms. Carpenter," Ms. Church said sternly, though she was smiling at the same time. She checked her list again. "As for you, your new husband will be Mr. Owen."

I gulped, feeling sorry for Wendell. Somehow I didn't think his new wife was going to love, honor, and cherish him—even for a few days. Sure enough, Marissa looked disgruntled, especially when Jake started laughing so hard that he almost choked.

I glanced at Wendell, who was keeping his eyes on his desk. Then my gaze shifted to Andie Foster. She was looking at Wendell with a sympathetic, caring expression that made her look prettier than ever. My heart skipped a beat. *What if . . .*

But before I could finish, Ms. Church pointed again. My heart skipped a beat, because I thought it was my turn. But she was actually looking past me at Kyle. "Mr. Bladen," she said, "your new wife will be Ms. Calhoun."

Courtney gasped loudly. "Sweetie!" she exclaimed, gazing happily at Kyle. "We're married!"

Kyle grinned and blew a kiss across the aisle to his girlfriend. "Cool. Good deal, Ms. Church. Thanks."

"Don't thank me yet." Ms. Church smiled. "I just figured the two of you might as well see what marriage is really like."

Ms. Church assigned several more couples, and I was starting to think she'd forgotten about me. After all, I was new—what if I wasn't on her list at all? Could I have counted wrong just now—could I be a leftover? I started counting again, feeling anxious.

"Ms. Foster."

I gulped. Ms. Church's voice had just totally

broken my concentration. Who would get matched up with Andie Foster the angel? *Probably Fuzzy,* I thought, realizing he hadn't been assigned a partner yet. *Those jocks have all the luck. They'll probably get along so well that he'll ask her to that Valentine's Day dance, and then—*

"Mr. Parker? Earth to Mr. Parker."

I suddenly realized that Ms. Church was standing in the aisle beside my table, peering at me and repeating my name. I blushed furiously. "Er—yes? Sorry. Um, what?"

Beside me, Jake snorted with laughter. "Hey, I don't blame you for being stunned, man," he said. "You got matched with the famous Andie Foster!"

There were a few nervous giggles at his words. But I hardly heard them. My heart was soaring as Ms. Church handed me an egg. She'd initialed each one, so we couldn't replace it if it broke. The egg felt smooth and solid in my hand.

I stared at it, not even really sure why I was so psyched. Sure, Andie was cute—beyond cute, really. But Veronica and Marissa were cute too. And I knew I wouldn't have this reaction if I'd been matched with one of them. Still, I decided not to fight it. This was my chance to get to know Andie better. Who knew what could happen?

I glanced up at her table with a tentative smile. Andie was looking back at me, her face serious and thoughtful.

Then Jake leaned over and punched me in the

shoulder. "Way to go, man," he whispered loudly enough for the entire class to hear.

I turned to grin at him. *So he thinks Andie's cute too,* I thought, feeling pleased. *I guess any guy would.*

But when I twisted back to smile again at Andie, she had turned away. She didn't look my way for the rest of the class period.

Finally the bell rang and I headed up to Andie's table, slinging my backpack over one shoulder and holding the egg carefully in my other hand. Wendell glanced at me and mumbled hello before gathering up his books and marching toward Marissa, looking like a prisoner headed to his own execution. But I barely bothered to nod in return. My attention was all on Andie.

She was even cuter up close. Her straight blond hair was loose today, falling over her shoulders and wisping around her face. This close, I saw that her eyes were a clear, soft blue, like a newborn kitten's.

"Hi," I said, suddenly feeling a little flustered. "Er, I'm Andy Parker. Looks like we're partners."

She didn't look up. Instead she kept fiddling with her backpack, sliding her books into the large compartment. "Looks like," she answered.

"Um, so we probably should talk about what we're going to do," I said, confused by her neutral, almost cold tone. It was totally at odds with her soft, vulnerable face. Had she seen through me, even though the others hadn't? Had she recognized the nerd within? "Work out a schedule or whatever."

"I guess." She sounded as though spending time with me was equal to a visit to the orthodontist.

I felt a wash of humiliation, and Amber's face popped into my head for a second. I banished her image quickly, focusing on Andie. "Uh, maybe we could meet up after school." I stumbled over my words. The cool Andy Parker was losing it fast.

"I work at the university library after school," she said bluntly. "We'll have to make it later."

"You work at the university library? Cool!"

As soon as the words left my mouth, I wished I could take them back. Talk about a nerd alert! What kind of guy sounded thrilled about hanging around a bunch of moldy old books?

However, when Andie responded, she sounded slightly less hostile. "Yeah," she said. "I work in the history wing."

I was relieved that she didn't seem repulsed by my overenthusiastic comment. To be honest, I really did think the university library was pretty amazing. My mom had taken me to campus a couple of times to show me around. The library was in an ancient stone building, four stories high, with all kinds of weirdly shaped rooms, half-hidden passageways, and even a couple of turrets. And books, of course. More books than I'd ever seen in one place. I could have spent months there, just wandering around and browsing through the stacks.

"Well, no problem," I told her. "I could meet you at the main desk when you're finished working. How does that sound?"

"Will Jake and the rest of the *guys* be with you?" Her voice had hardened up again, the words sounding icy and bitter.

"No," I answered, puzzled. "Just me. Is that okay? I mean, if there's a problem . . ."

"No, it's nothing." Her voice was neutral this time. "Look, I get off at seven-thirty today. See you then, okay?"

"Okay." I watched as she hurried out of the room without a backward glance. Glancing down at the egg in my hand, I shrugged. "Guess I'm taking first shift with Junior," I murmured.

Jake was waiting for me outside of the classroom. "Way to go, man! You scored big-time. I'd like to know why new guys have all the luck."

The way Jake was jumping around in his excitement, I was afraid my new baby egg was in danger. I carefully tucked it into an outside pocket of my backpack, hoping that my spare pair of gym socks would cushion it a little. "I know," I told Jake. "Andie seems great."

Jake grinned at me, his brown eyes dancing mischievously. "Yeah, great. So how does it feel, man? You get to *couple* with Andie Foster. Oops! I mean *be* a couple, of course." He laughed loudly and winked at me.

I wasn't sure what was so funny, and it made me a little nervous. Jake was acting pretty weird. Was it some kind of jock thing that I didn't know about? Was this the way normal guys always talked to each other about girls? "Um, sure. And Andie sure is pretty, isn't she?"

"Come on, man. It's me, Jake." Suddenly his jaw dropped and he smacked himself on the side of the head. "Dude! Could it be you haven't heard about your new wife?"

"Heard what?"

Jake gave me a grin that was more like a leer. "Andie Foster hasn't been at Fairview very long," he said. "But she's already made a *lot* of friends. *Good* friends. If you know what I mean."

I was starting to think I knew exactly what he meant. But I couldn't believe it. "What are you saying? Do you mean she's, uh . . ." I blushed.

"Friendly," Jake finished for me, drawing the word out suggestively. "Man, I'm telling you—you play your cards right, and you'll be doing more than playing house with her."

Jake and I wandered down the hall toward our next class. I was in shock, trying to take in what Jake was telling me. Still, I could tell that I had gone up a couple of notches in my new friend's eyes, just as a result of being paired up with Andie. I definitely didn't want to blow that by challenging what he was saying. But I had to find out the truth. "So is this for real?" I asked carefully. "I mean, you know how guys can be."

"I know how *Andie* can be." He wiggled his eyebrows at me with a lewd grin.

I gulped. "You mean you . . . ?"

"Well, no," Jake admitted quickly. "I mean, I could have, you know? But I was dating, uh, someone at the time." His gaze skittered across the hall to where Marissa was standing by the water fountain talking to Lauren Epps. "So I didn't want to—well, you know. But I could have." He shrugged. "From what I hear, just about *anyone* could have."

I might have been a geek in my previous life, but I wasn't totally clueless. I knew how guys talked. If Jake hadn't been with Andie himself, how could he possibly know for sure that she was sleeping with other guys?

Where there's smoke, there's fire. The old saying popped into my head before I could stop it. I shook my head, feeling confused.

"Yo!" Fuzzy caught up with us, clapping his big hands onto our shoulders. "Dudes. Did either of you finish the chapter for history class?"

Jake spun around and grabbed Fuzzy's arm. "Hey, man," he said. "What do you think of Parker's new psych partner?"

Fuzzy glanced at me. "Huh?" Suddenly his face cleared, and I could almost see the lightbulb flickering on above his head. "Oh!" he exclaimed with a grin. "Yeah. Foxy Foster. Pretty good deal, dude. Gotta love *that* homework."

I was starting to feel annoyed with them. Andie seemed really nice. If the guys were going to trash her, I thought they should at least be sure about their facts.

Fuzzy was chuckling by now. "Lucky you," he said, pounding me on the back. "You're made in the shade, bro."

"Yeah," Jake put in with a smirk. "At least *somebody* will be getting some."

40

"What's that supposed to mean, dillweed?" Fuzzy stopped laughing and scowled at Jake.

Jake shrugged, still smiling. "Hey, it could happen to anyone, man." He glanced at me. "He bombed out big-time up in Michigan this weekend. Even his cousin's wild roommate shot him down."

"Oh, yeah?" Fuzzy challenged him. "Well, I didn't see you getting any action up there either. Besides, who are you to talk about me? You couldn't even score with Andie Foster."

This was getting out of hand. Not to mention off the subject. "Hold it," I said with an authority I didn't really feel. But they both stopped glaring at each other and turned to me. "What are you saying, Fuzzy? Have you been with Andie? For real?"

"You calling me a liar?" Fuzzy raised an eyebrow and took a step toward me.

I gulped. I'm not short, but he towered over me. "No way," I said quickly. "It was just a question, man. Really."

Fuzzy nodded, seeming appeased. "Yeah," he said. "Last fall, right after she moved here." He shrugged. "It was no big deal. We only did the deed maybe four, five times. Then I decided it was time to move on."

"Yeah, but the old Fuzzman gave her a taste for it." Jake seemed to have forgotten already that he and his friend had practically come to blows only seconds earlier. He slapped Fuzzy on the back, looking proud. "After he got through with her, she moved on to another guy, and then another, and then . . . well, you get the picture."

Fuzzy nodded. "She must've had four guys in the first month. Including a couple of buddies of mine." He shook his head. "Total nympho. Like I said, dude, you've got it made."

The bell rang before I could answer, its shrill buzz making me jump. The three of us took off, racing into our history classroom just before the teacher arrived. But I spent the entire class brooding about what the guys had just told me.

Could it be true? I sneaked a glance at Fuzzy. He wasn't paying attention to the teacher either. Instead he was leaning on his desk making lecherous faces at a cute girl whose name I didn't know. She was giggling and waving at him in return.

Why would Fuzzy make up stories about Andie? He was a member of the jock crowd—a star of the football team. He could have just about any girl in the school. Why pick on someone who'd just moved to town?

Unless it's true, a little voice in my head finished. *Unless everything they say about Andie really happened.*

By the time class finally ended, my stomach was twisted into knots. "Yo, Parker," Jake said, gathering up his books. "Ready to hit the caf?"

The last thing I wanted to think about was lunch. "I'll catch up with you," I told Jake and Fuzzy. "I need to make a pit stop."

I headed to the boys' bathroom. Nobody else was there, so I just leaned on the sink for a moment, staring at myself in the mirror. The new and improved Andy Parker stared back at me—complete with contact lenses, cool haircut, and carefully chosen clothes. But inside I still felt like the old Andrew Jackson Parker.

Get a grip, I told myself. *You're getting exactly what you wanted. Jake and the guys are treating you like a friend. And who knows what will happen with Andie? No sense getting all worked up about it before you even get to know her.*

That made me feel a little better. Maybe Fuzzy was full of it, maybe not. All I could do was wait and see. Get to know Andie better. Then I could judge the truth for myself.

That sounds like a plan, I thought, turning on the cold-water tap and leaning over to splash my face. *Innocent until proven guilty, right?*

I raised my dripping face, glancing over as I grabbed a paper towel from the dispenser on the wall. As I did, I noticed some graffiti scrawled in blue pen across the wall beside the mirror: *Looking to lose your virginity, losers? Call Andie Foster!*

Four

"HI, HONEY," MY mom called from the living room as I let myself into the house that afternoon. "How was school?"

I dropped my coat on the bench in the front hallway and poked my head into the room. "Hi, Mom," I said, trying to sound normal. "It was fine."

"Good." Mom pushed her wire-rimmed glasses back up on her nose and glanced down at the stack of papers on the coffee table in front of her. "Your dad's on a conference call with his editor, but he said he'll start dinner as soon as he's finished. And I just have a few more of these tests to get through."

"Okay," I said. "Well, I'd better get started on my homework."

Mom nodded and ran one hand through her wild, frizzy grayish brown hair, making it stick up

44

even more. She looked really busy, and for a moment I was tempted to offer my help. I'd always liked playing teaching assistant. But I figured that today I'd be too nervous to be much help. All I could think about was meeting Andie at the library in a couple of hours.

I headed upstairs, leaving the living room to Mom. She had a huge home office above the garage that she shared with Dad, but she hardly ever seemed to use it. Personally, I suspected that all the bizarre souvenirs that Dad brought back from his South American research trips every year gave her the creeps. I mean, we're talking giant dried beetles, scary-looking tribal masks—the works. The weirder the better—that was Dad's motto, at least when it came to mementos.

My room was kind of scary in a different way. As I opened the door, I glanced around. There was my poster of great Russian chess players, right next to a framed picture of the starship *Enterprise* that had been signed by several *Star Trek* cast members. The trombone I'd played briefly in second and third grades was hanging on the wall over my bed. My very first real microscope—a gift from my parents on my eighth birthday—was tucked away on a shelf beside my complete collection of *Mad* magazines. My grandfather's chess set occupied most of the desk under the window.

Somehow my transformation into cool Andy Parker hadn't quite made it to my room. True, a baseball bat leaned in a corner, with a glove and ball sitting on the bookshelf nearby. Still, I couldn't quite imagine what Jake, Fuzzy, and Kyle might say if they stopped by.

I guess I'll have to do something about this place, I thought, flopping onto my bed. I pulled the egg—I'd started thinking of it as Andy junior—out of my backpack, relieved to see that it was still in one piece. I stared at it, my heart thumping nervously. *But that can wait. First I have to figure out what I'm going to say to Andie.*

I walked into the main reception area of the library promptly at seven-thirty, but Andie was already there waiting for me. Actually, she was perched on the edge of the returns desk, bending over a book. Her back was to me, and the sweater she was wearing was riding up a little, exposing a couple of inches of her back.

I just stared for a moment, mesmerized by the curve of her spine. I'd had no idea a back could be so sexy.

She glanced up and saw me. Our eyes connected and held, and she blushed. Then she frowned. "I'm almost finished," she snapped, sounding almost angry. "I'll get my bag and jacket."

I waited for her, wondering about the weird reaction. Had she realized I was staring at her like a lovesick puppy? I sure hoped not. But I hadn't been able to help it.

Soon she was back, slinging her backpack over

her shoulder. "Feel like hitting the Shop 'n' Save?" she asked. "We need to check out the food prices so we can start on our budget."

"Uh, good idea," I said, realizing that I hadn't thought about the project at all. I'd been too busy dreaming about spending time with Andie. "Should we make up a shopping list?"

"Done," she replied, fishing a sheet of notebook paper out of her bag and handing it over.

I scanned it quickly. Milk, bread, diapers, et cetera. Your basic married-with-egg shopping list, as far as I could tell. "Okay, then—what are we waiting for?" I said. "Let's hit the store."

I stood back to let her go first when we reached the exit. As we walked away from the library, I glanced over my shoulder. The library building loomed behind us, looking cool and mysterious and romantic, as it always did. "Hey," I said. "It must be pretty cool working here, huh?"

She shrugged. "It's a job," she said. But from the tone of her voice, I suspected that it was more than that.

But I didn't push it. "Okay," I said as we hit the sidewalk marking the edge of the campus. Fairview was small enough to put almost everything within walking distance when the weather was decent, so I hadn't bothered to bring my car. "Still, it definitely beats flipping burgers. How'd you land such a great job when you just moved here?"

She shot me an unreadable glance. "They gave

me a shot because I worked at the public library in my old hometown. How did you know I just moved here?"

Embarrassed at the slipup, I tried to wave it off. "I hear things."

She frowned, and I realized that was exactly the wrong thing to say. Lots of "things" were said about Andie Foster.

I searched for a way to smooth over the awkward silence. "Uh, so you work in the history section, huh? That must be a little, well, boring." I got straight A's in history like in everything else, but it had never been my favorite subject.

Andie laughed. "Actually, I love history," she said. "It's fun finding out the stories behind stuff, you know? Like how people used to live in the old days, or what famous leaders were like in their early years."

"I guess." I'd never really looked at it that way. She made it sound fun—like a good movie or something. "Anyway, my parents would definitely agree with you. They're scientists by trade— Mom's a math professor, and Dad is a behavioral scientist—but they're both major history buffs. That's how I ended up being named Andrew Jackson Parker."

"Really? That's your name?" She turned to study my face, then smiled. "I don't know. I don't see you as an Andrew Jackson."

I shrugged. "Hey, me neither," I said, sort of wishing I'd never brought up this whole topic.

The last thing I wanted was for the other kids at school to find out my full name. Pretty geeky stuff. "That's why I go by Andy."

She was still looking at me appraisingly. "I'm not sure I see you as an Andy either," she said thoughtfully. Then, as if realizing what she'd said, she laughed and averted her gaze. "Oh. I mean, well . . . whatever. Look, there's the supermarket."

Sure enough, we had arrived. We passed the line of shopping carts at the entrance and headed inside. Even the perpetual chill of the produce section felt cozy after the brisk evening air outside. "Okay," I said. "Let's get started. Where do they keep the milk?"

She shot me a suspicious glance. "You're kidding, right? You must not do much grocery shopping."

I shrugged. "I guess I don't. Mom takes care of that stuff."

"Well, don't expect *this* wife to be just like Mom in that way." She grinned and poked me in the arm. "This is going to be a liberated marriage. That means hubby helps with everything. Shopping, taking care of the baby, cooking . . ."

"Uh-oh," I joked as we wandered down the wide aisle, pausing now and then to jot down a price. "I'm not sure I like what you're saying there. I once set the toaster on fire trying to heat up a couple of Pop-Tarts."

She giggled. "You didn't."

"I did," I said, crossing my heart. "So I'm really, really hoping you can cook."

Laughing again, she nodded. "Don't worry. I wouldn't say I'm Julia Child or anything, but I can whip up something edible when I have to." She leaned over to check the price on a tub of butter, then straightened up and glanced at me. "Actually, I wind up cooking a lot when Mom's on the evening shift. She's a manager at one of the department stores in the mall."

I nodded. "What does your dad do?"

I winced as soon as the words left my mouth, realizing that her dad might not be around. Might be dead, even. *Nice going, Parker,* I thought. *Very smooth. Tactful, even.*

But Andie didn't seem to mind. She shrugged. "He and Mom split up when I was just a toddler. He got married again and had another family, and now he lives in California. I don't see him all that often."

"Do you miss him?" I asked.

"Sometimes." She shrugged again. "Whatever. So, what about you? Are your parents together?'

"Yeah," I answered. "They're weird like that."

"Maybe your dad should do a behavioral study of himself and figure it out."

We both laughed. Andie had a nice laugh— sort of musical and free and eager, like it was just waiting to get out of her. I decided I could listen to that laugh all day.

"Hey," she said, pointing to something on the

refrigerated shelf nearby. "I forgot to put eggs on the shopping list."

"Eggs?" I pretended to look horrified. "For Junior? But that's cannibalism!"

That brought out the musical laugh again. "Shouldn't that be, um, *eggibalism?*" she joked.

"No, no," I corrected. "I think the proper term is *canneggilism.*"

We laughed together for a minute or two over that. I know, I know, it was a pretty lame joke when you get right down to it. But it was just the moment—Andie and me, goofing around together. Being silly. Like friends.

Finally we settled down and continued our shopping, moving on to the milk and then turning to seek out the cereal aisle. My thoughts returned to our previous line of conversation. "You know, I guess I am pretty lucky with the parents I have," I said. "They're pretty cool. They let me do my own thing most of the time. Although sometimes they do like to lecture me about being responsible and grown-up."

"I know that feeling." Andie nodded, her expression thoughtful and a little distant. "Mom works so hard and I'm home alone so much that sometimes I feel like I always have to be really grown-up. Know what I mean?"

"Yeah," I said, though I wasn't sure that I did. What exactly did she mean by being grown-up?

She changed the subject back to our project then, and I did my best to focus. Meanwhile, we were still making our way through the store. Luckily for me, Andie was doing most of the writing, marking down prices on her shopping list, because I was totally distracted. Her mention of being home alone so much had started me thinking about things that I really didn't want to think about. Especially right then, when we were getting along so well.

"Andy?" She smiled at me and brushed my arm with her hand. "Earth to Andy. Did you hear what I said about the pork chops?"

"Uh, what?" My skin tingled where she'd touched it. I stared down at my arm, feeling my face turning pink. Was she just being friendly and concerned, or did her touching me mean more?

Get a grip, Parker! I chided myself. *You're freaking yourself out for no reason. Just chill, or Andie's going to think you're an even bigger freak than you actually are.*

"Sorry," I managed in a more normal tone as we turned down the baby-supply aisle. "I guess I spaced for a second. What did you say?"

Before she could answer, I heard Jake call my name. Glancing up, I saw him hurrying toward us from the other end of the aisle, Fuzzy at his heels. "Yo, Parker!" he said again, a big grin on his face. He turned toward Andie. "And this must be the little woman."

Fuzzy was grinning too. "Hey, you two. Been getting lots of practice making babies?" He grabbed a baby bottle shaped like a puppy off the shelf nearby and waved it in Andie's face.

Andie's face looked like it was set in stone. I could tell it was taking a lot of effort for her to ignore them. She turned away and copied down the price from a box of diapers.

Jake and Fuzzy continued to kid around, making really lame and not-too-subtle jokes at Andie's expense. I knew they really didn't mean any harm, but it was obvious that Andie was really uncomfortable. Finally I decided it was time to step in. "Hey, guys, we're trying to work here." I was careful to keep my tone light. "Don't you have wives of your own to bother?"

Fuzzy frowned. "Oh, yeah," he muttered, glancing over his shoulder with a guilty look on his face. I almost laughed out loud. Fuzzy's partner was a really smart, studious, and rather bossy girl named Joanne.

Jake leaned closer to Andie, getting right up in her face. "Yeah," he said. "Listen, honey. Feel free to give Veronica any little wifely pointers you want, huh? I'm starting to realize she could use some loosening up. And you're just the girl to help her with that, right? *Loose*." He drew out the last word with a meaningful smirk.

Andie stiffened and turned away, and Jake snorted with laughter. "Catch ya in the A.M., bro," he said to me. "If you're not too exhausted from all this . . . shopping." He leered at Andie before turning away.

I rolled my eyes. Jake was a cool guy in most

ways, but I was starting to realize that he could be a little immature when it came to girls. "Ready to roll?" I asked Andie, trying to keep my voice light. No sense making her feel worse than she already did about Jake's silly comments.

She just stared at me for a second, her face ashen. Then she turned and ran.

I caught up with her halfway across the parking lot. "Hey, Andie, wait up," I called. Putting on one last burst of speed, I managed to grab her arm, spinning her toward me.

"Let go of me!" She pulled her arm away, and I let go, shocked at how angry she sounded. Then I saw her face and realized she was holding back tears.

Feeling uncomfortable, I tried to laugh it off. I had absolutely no idea what to do. "The guys were just being stupid. Don't pay any attention to them."

"Guys will be guys?" she said bitterly. "Yeah, well, I guess I shouldn't have expected anything different from you, considering that they're your friends." She turned to walk away from me, but I caught her arm again.

"This is only my third day of school," I said. "I've had lunch with Jake and his friends a couple of times and hung out a little. But that doesn't mean I'm just like them."

"Whatever."

I could tell she didn't believe me. I bit my lip, not sure what to say next. *I'm not like them,* I could say. *I'm not cool—I'm a chess-obsessed,* Star Trek*-watching, calculus-loving geekazoid.*

Yeah, right. Andie might not be crazy about me as Jake's buddy, but things would only be worse if she knew the real Andrew Jackson Parker, king of the nerds. I remembered Amber's words to me once again and flushed. Andie would never understand.

"Look," I said helplessly, "Jake can be a jerk. No question about it. But you can't just assume I'm the same way because I hang out with him sometimes. That's not fair."

It was a pretty lame argument, but she glanced at me, looking uncertain. "Well . . ." She hesitated. "That's true."

"Can I walk you home?" I asked.

She considered me for a moment and then nodded grudgingly. Without saying anything, we fell into step together. I remained silent as she blew her nose. She didn't seem quite so mad anymore, but she also didn't seem eager to chat.

We walked a long way in silence. Finally, feeling desperate to prove that I wasn't the creep she thought I was, I started a conversation about a history paper I'd written freshman year about the invention of the printing press. That seemed to do the trick. We chatted about history and books and other neutral topics for the next few blocks, until finally Andie stopped on the sidewalk in front of a small but well-kept frame house.

"Here we are," Andie said, gesturing at the house. "Home sweet home."

"It's nice," I said, meaning it. The house was small—the whole thing probably could have fit into my family's two-car garage—but it had a lot of charm. Gingerbread decorated the front porch, bright curtains were visible behind the windows, and the front walk was lined with small lights that had already come on against the dark evening sky. "Very nice."

"Thanks." She paused, scuffing her boot toe on the sidewalk. "So anyway, I told my mom about our project," she said, not quite meeting my eye. "She called me at work to say she'd be home late tonight."

I gulped. Was this her way of letting me know that she was . . . *available?* That she wanted me to make some kind of move? I glanced at the house again, feeling my stomach clench nervously.

Andie didn't seem to notice my consternation. "Anyway," she went on, "she cracked up when I told her your name." I guess I must have been staring at her blankly, because she smiled and added, "Andy and Andie."

"Oh!" I said. "Right. Andy and Andie. Pretty funny." I realized I hadn't really thought about it. Probably because I still thought of myself as Andrew, not Andy.

"Yeah," she said. "But it could get confusing, you know? So I was thinking, maybe we should give you a nickname."

"Me? Why not you?"

She shrugged. "Because you're the new guy. If I was going to have a nickname, I'd already have one."

You do, I thought, feeling my cheeks start to burn as I thought of all the names my new friends had for her.

"Um, so, any ideas?" I asked quickly to cover my thoughts.

"Well, let's see." She put one finger to her chin as she thought. She looked adorable when she did that. "Andrew Jackson Parker. How about Jack?"

"I don't think so."

"Okay, okay. How about A.J.? You know, for Andrew Jackson."

"A.J." I tried it out. "Not bad. I could probably live with that." I felt ridiculously pleased. I'd never really had a nickname before—not unless you count Brain or Doofus or Nerd Boy.

"Good." She smiled, making my heart palpitate strangely. "We've successfully negotiated our first compromise as a married couple. I'll include it in our log."

She looked so cute when she smiled that way that I had a wild, crazy impulse to lean down and kiss her right then and there. I could almost feel her lips against mine, feel her beating heart pressed against my chest. . . . But I seemed to be frozen in place. I couldn't move a muscle. All I could do was gaze at her, memorizing every inch of her face.

"Um, so what should we do next?" she asked. "I mean, for our project," she added quickly, looking a little embarrassed. I wondered if there was any way she could have guessed what I was thinking. "Maybe you could come over tomorrow night and meet Mom. You know, for the getting-along-with-the-in-laws thing. It's the only night she's off this week."

She smiled at me shyly, and I felt my heart flip-flop. For a moment I forgot all about her wild reputation. All I could see was the amazing, beautiful, interesting person standing there in front of me. "Sure," I said, trying not to sound as eager as I felt. "Tomorrow night would be great."

Five

I FLOATED THROUGH the next day at school, living for the moments when I might pass Andie in the hall and say hi. She'd taken Junior home with her last night and passed him to me after homeroom.

I was ready. I'd borrowed this weird little box my dad brought home from his last trip—wooden, with a sliding cover—and packed it with cotton balls, making the perfect little bed for Junior. Andie had seemed impressed with my efforts, which made them all worthwhile. I couldn't wait to hang out with her again that afternoon.

By the time I needed to leave for Andie's house, snow had started to fall outside. I grabbed my heavy parka out of the closet by the back door and headed for the front hall to get my boots. I was pulling them on, humming under my breath, when my mom walked by.

She stopped and looked at me. "My little boy—off to meet his in-laws!" She straightened my shirt collar.

"Yeah, right, Mom," I said, rolling my eyes at the lame joke, but smiling at the same time. I playfully slapped her hand away from my collar. "And please, I'm a married man, remember? I can dress myself."

She stepped back from me. "I was just admiring how tall and handsome you've grown. Is that a new shirt?"

Sometimes my parents were a little slow on the uptake—okay, sometimes glaciers moved faster. "I thought I'd try a new look for my new school."

"Oh." She gave me a quizzical stare, like I was a challenging math problem she was trying to solve. Then she shrugged and glanced out the window. "Wow, it's really starting to come down out there. You'd better put on a hat and scarf."

"Okay." I knew better than to argue. I even let her wrap the scarf around my neck, bundling me up so tight I could hardly breathe.

I left, carrying Junior, and walked over to Andie's house. I knocked on the door and then stomped my feet to shake off the snow and warm myself up. It was well below freezing, and even my suffocating scarf hadn't totally kept away the chill.

Then Andie opened the door and smiled at me. Suddenly I felt nice and toasty warm. "Come in," she said, stepping back to let me pass. "Let me take your coat."

"Thanks," I said. At least, that was what I meant to say. It came out more like "Mmmfmmpfs," thanks to that stupid scarf.

I grabbed one end of it and yanked, thinking I could pull it off with one motion. But Mom had done a pretty thorough wrapping job. All I managed to do was make the scarf tighter and almost strangle myself.

Andie laughed. "Here," she said, "let me help you with that." She came closer and began to unwind the scarf from around my face.

Once again I found myself unable to breathe, but this time it had nothing to do with the scarf. I was very aware of how close she was—the curve of her cheek, the scent of her shampoo, the tendrils of blond hair around her temples moving gently in the breeze from the heating vent all assaulted my senses, making me feel weird and fuzzy inside.

After a second she too seemed to notice how close we were. She blinked and glanced up, and her fingers on my scarf shook slightly.

Does she want me to kiss her? I wondered. *Is that why she's standing so close?*

The thought terrified me and excited me at the same time. But I couldn't seem to think about where it might lead. All I could think about was leaning over, taking her in my arms, and feeling her lips meet mine. I bent my head slightly, moving my mouth toward hers. But my lips were still a good six inches short of their goal when she sort of gasped and jumped backward, away from me.

Unfortunately, she was still holding on to my scarf. Her sudden move yanked it tighter around my neck, pulling me off balance. "Ulp!" I gurgled, grabbing for the scarf with one hand and wind-milling the other, trying to stay upright.

"Oops!" she exclaimed, stepping forward at the same time to help. Instead she managed to put her foot down right in front of mine, tripping me and sending me flying—right into her. Before I knew what had happened, the two of us had hurtled across the tiny foyer in a tangle of arms and legs, fi-nally coming to rest in a small armchair. I found myself staring down at Andie, who was pinned be-neath my body.

"Oh!" I quickly pulled myself off her and stood, offering a hand to help her up. "Are you okay? I'm really sorry."

Her cheeks burned scarlet. "Yes, I'm fine. And you don't have to apologize—it was my fault."

"Andie!" a woman's voice called from another room. "Are you bringing your friend inside, or are you keeping him out in the cold all night long?"

"We're coming, Mom!" Andie called back, seeming relieved at the interruption. I knew exactly how she felt.

I followed her into the kitchen at the back of the house. I was sort of nervous about meeting Andie's mother. But Mrs. Foster turned out to be really nice. She was just about the opposite of my mother in looks—slim and stylishly dressed, with the same straight, pale blond hair as Andie. But for some reason she still reminded me a little of Mom. Maybe it was because she seemed so warm and open and real. I could tell that she and Andie had a great relationship. They had an easy rapport and were good at teasing each other, but always with a hint of fondness.

As I sat there, watching Andie kid around with her mother, it was getting harder and harder to believe that she could be the same girl that Fuzzy and the guys had told me about. How could she seem so sweet and nice and, yes, innocent, and still have done all the things they said she did? It didn't compute.

After we finished eating, Mrs. Foster disappeared into the kitchen to clean up while Andie and I headed into the den to work on our project.

As we sat there on the couch going over the chart Ms. Church had given us, there was no hint that Andie was thinking about anything but our project. She certainly wasn't giving me any indication that she wanted to jump my bones.

Get a clue, Parker, I thought. *Maybe you were on to something before. Maybe she can tell you're a geek at heart. Maybe she just wants to be pals with you. Maybe you don't rate like Fuzzy and those other guys do.*

The Valentine's Day dance was just around the corner. Was I being a fool to imagine taking Andie as my date? I imagined slow-dancing with her, smelling the floral scent of her shampoo, running my hands over her back . . .

But what if the stories were true? It didn't stop me from wanting to spend time with her. But if she expected a lot more than dancing from me, I wasn't sure I was ready to deliver. I mean, guys were always supposed to want to go all the way, but I wasn't like that. Well, okay, maybe I was like that—but I definitely didn't want to get into anything so intense with a girl until I got to know her first. I wanted to be in love with her and know that she was in love with me. Even then, I kind of liked the idea of taking it slow.

We were working on our family budget when Mrs. Foster emerged from the kitchen bearing a couple of plates. "Dessert time! I thought you could use a study break—pie and ice cream."

"Thanks, Mom," Andie said.

"Yeah, thanks, Mrs. Foster," I added. The pie smelled great. As Mrs. Foster left the room again, Andie and I dug in, and soon our plates were practically licked clean.

I leaned back on the couch and sighed contentedly. "That was awesome," I said. "Tell your mom she's an amazing cook."

"Sure." Andie smiled. "I just hope I can live up to that when it's time to cook our family meal."

"I'm sure whatever you cook will be great."

I guess the words came out a little more intense than I'd meant them, because she blushed and looked away for a moment. "Um, I think this budget is just about finished," she said after a long pause.

"Really?" I said, a little too quickly. "That wasn't too bad. What a relief! The way Ms. Church talks, marriage sounds like the hardest thing in the world."

"Yeah?" Andie shrugged, her blue eyes distant. "Well, sometimes I think high school is the hardest thing we're ever going to have to get through."

I glanced over at her, surprised by her suddenly serious tone. "Really?"

She was still gazing off into space at something I couldn't see. "I mean, everything can be going along okay, and then you make one mistake—or one decision that doesn't even seem like a mistake at the time—and everyone turns on you."

I guessed that Andie was thinking about her own reputation. I wasn't sure what to say. Did she want me to ask her about it? Or did she think I was still so new that I didn't know what the other guys said about her?

Before I could decide what to say, she'd turned away to tuck the budget into the pocket of her notebook. I watched as she bent over her notebook, a lock of white-blond hair falling forward over her shoulder and the buttery light from the table lamp lighting up the soft pink blush of her cheek.

I didn't think about what I was going to do next. I just let my impulses take over. Leaning forward, I took her chin gently in one hand and kissed her. Her lips tasted sweetly of apple pie and vanilla ice cream. I moved in closer, sliding my hand from her chin to the back of her neck and sinking further into the kiss, pressing my lips against hers a little harder. She made a funny noise in the back of her throat and pushed me away.

I gulped, feeling a little dizzy as I sat back and blinked at her. She touched her lips with her hand and looked at me with surprise. Surprise, and a shadow of another emotion . . . "Why did you do that?" she choked out.

"Um, I–I'm sorry," I stammered. This wasn't exactly the reaction I was hoping for. "I like you, Andie. I just wanted to show you that." She was still staring at me with that weird expression in her eyes. As if she wasn't sure who I was or why I was there. Did that mean she didn't like me the way I liked her?

"It's getting late," Andie said, not quite meeting my eyes. "I should probably get started on my other homework."

I knew a hint when I heard one. "Yeah, you're right," I said, standing up. "So, what do you want to do tomorrow?"

"How about the housework stuff?" she suggested, heading toward the front door without looking at me. "I get off work at the library at five-thirty. You could come over here after that and we could clean the house." She finally glanced up at me with her blue, blue eyes. "Mom has to work until midnight, so we'll have plenty of time. And it would be a nice surprise for her to come home to a clean house."

I gulped. Was I being paranoid, or had Andie made a real point of letting me know that we could be alone together for the whole evening? Just when I thought we were really starting to connect, things had got weird again. First she acted as though she was sorry I'd kissed her, and then in the next breath she invited me over to spend time alone with her in her house. I was dizzy with trying to figure it all out.

"Uh, okay," I said, trying to sound cool. "That would be fine." I wished I had the guts to kiss her again. But she was keeping her eyes trained on the floor as she opened the door to let me out. So I just cleared my throat and patted her awkwardly on the arm. "See you tomorrow."

It was still snowing lightly when I stepped outside, and the flakes melted against my face. As I walked toward my neighborhood, I realized I was too keyed up to go straight home. Glancing around, I remembered a neon sign I'd spotted a couple of blocks away. Moe's Burgers. Wasn't that the place Jake had mentioned? I figured I might as well check it out. Maybe a milk shake and some fries would help settle the butterflies that started up in my stomach every time I thought about that kiss.

Moe's Burgers was warm and noisy and brightly lit and packed with kids from Fairview High. I walked in, brushing the snow off my hair and feeling a little nervous. A couple of guys sitting at the counter turned to shoot me curious looks, and I thought I saw a girl over by the jukebox nod toward me as she leaned over to whisper something to her friend.

What am I doing here? I wondered. *I may be*

cooler than I used to be, but am I really ready for this?

"Yo!" Jake's familiar voice rose above the din. "Parker! Dude!"

I turned and saw him crowded into a booth with Fuzzy, Kyle, Courtney, and Marissa. I hurried over to them, feeling relieved to be rescued from my own insecurity.

"Where've you been, man?" Jake asked me, crowding against Marissa to make room on the end of the seat. "We stopped by your house earlier to see if you wanted to catch a movie or something, but nobody was home."

My heart leaped. Jake and the guys had stopped by for me? "I had dinner at Andie Foster's house. As part of our psych project," I added hurriedly when I saw the smirk on the others' faces.

"Bet she served something really tasty," Marissa drawled.

"Her mother was there," I said firmly, feeling a sudden need to defend Andie.

"Brent Carver said that never stopped Andie before." Jake leaned in closer. "So tell all. Did you get lucky?"

"Jake, you're a pig!" Courtney said. She turned to shoot me a sympathetic look. "You don't have to tell us anything, Andy."

Jake waved her words away as if he were shooing gnats. "Come on, Parker. How was she? I bet it was awesome, since she'd had so much experience."

I hesitated, facing five pairs of curious eyes.

Even though Courtney had come to my defense, it was clear that she had jumped to the same conclusion the others had.

The image of Andie's soft blue eyes popped into my head, looking at me trustingly as I bent down to kiss her. "No," I blurted. "Uh, I mean, uh . . ."

As I fumbled on, Kyle started to laugh. "Hey, it's okay, man," he said, slapping me on the back. "I guess you need some time to recover, huh?"

I shrugged weakly, not knowing what to say. They seemed determined to believe what they wanted to believe about Andie. How could I change their minds about her? Did I even want to change their minds? After all, it couldn't be hurting my rep as a cool guy to have everyone think I'd scored in my first week at school. Besides, I didn't even know for sure that the stories weren't true. What was I going on, anyway? A pair of pretty blue eyes and a couple of nice conversations?

Maybe I'm not leaping to her defense, I thought, slumping back against the seat as someone across the restaurant called to Fuzzy, distracting the others for a moment. *But at least I'm not telling stories about her like everyone else.*

That was a cop-out, and I knew it. I was starting to know Andie as a person. And I couldn't believe she would do all those things. I knew I should say something. Even if they didn't believe me, at least I could tell myself I'd tried.

But then the others started talking about a party they'd all gone to the previous month, and suddenly

I remembered that I'd really only known them for a few days.

I didn't want to blow my friendship with them. No way. Not when my high-school career finally seemed to be getting on track. There would be plenty of time to explain what Andie was really like. Just as soon as the time was right, when the guys would really believe me, I'd tell them the truth.

Six

ANDIE'S HOUSE WASN'T big, but it felt cavernous when I stepped inside the next afternoon. I was all too aware that it was just the two of us. But I tried to act normal as I looked around Andie's kitchen. She'd laid out more cleaning supplies than I'd ever known existed.

"Here." Andie passed me a mop. "Don't stand there looking confused. You can mop the floor. I'll turn the chairs upside down on the table so you can reach under it."

I felt like the world's biggest spoiled brat. "You know, I've never really done this before. . . ."

She laughed, her eyes crinkling a little at the corners. "Really?" she said. "Or are you just trying to trick me into doing all the dirty work?"

"Really," I said solemnly. "I'm totally clueless."

She gave me a quick lesson on the fine points of mopping. Once I was feeling a little more confident about my technique, she left to start vacuuming the living room.

After a while I really started getting into it. A few hours of mopping could seriously build up your arm muscles, I thought. Plus it was actually sort of relaxing at the same time. Swish. Back. Squeeze. Dip. Swish. Back. Squeeze . . .

"A.J., you're going to wear out the floor!"

I turned around to find Andie laughing at me from the doorway. "Huh?"

"You've been mopping for fifteen minutes. Every germ in town is on the run by now."

I grinned sheepishly, leaning the mop against the counter. "I just wanted to make sure I did a good job." I was still a little embarrassed that I was such a doofus when it came to housework. Andie seemed to be an expert. Of course, an only child growing up with a single mother probably had to take on a lot of adult responsibilities.

Which made me wonder. Having her father walk out on the family must have made Andie grow up kind of fast. What if she thought sex was just another normal part of being grown-up? *Stop it, Parker,* I told myself. *You're making yourself crazy. Just focus on what you're supposed to be doing and leave it at that.*

I swung my arms, stretching out my shoulder muscles. "What's next?" I asked, taking a step toward her.

"Look out!" she shouted. But it was too late. My foot connected with the handle of the mop and I went flying. So did the mop. It crashed into the bucket of water, knocking it over—just as I hit the floor. I was soaked instantly.

Once I'd caught my breath, I looked up to see Andie doubled over with laughter. "Very nice," I said, sitting up with a groan and squeezing about a quart of water out of my hair. It ran down my back in a cold stream. "Very sympathetic, Foster."

"Sorry." Her voice was weak with laughter. "I'm sorry. You just look so— Are you all right? You didn't hurt yourself, did you?"

I shook my head ruefully. "The only thing damaged is my pride, I think."

"Good." Andie gave one last giggle, then offered her hand to help me to my feet. Her hand felt warm and soft. "I'll get you something dry to wear."

She dropped my hand and hurried out of the room before I could answer. As I shook more soapy water off myself, I glanced through the doorway where she'd disappeared. *What would Jake do if he were in my place right now?* I wondered. *Would he just stand here like a doofus, or would he follow her upstairs? Use this situation as an opening?*

Before I could figure out what I was supposed to do—what I *wanted* to do—she returned. She was holding something behind her back, her eyes twinkling mischievously. Then she held it out: a pink chenille bathrobe with flowers sewn on it. I was a little dismayed. Was that supposed to be some kind of statement about how virile she found me? To cover my own embarrassment, I modeled the robe against my chest and looked at her questioningly.

She smiled and told me that it was practically a family heirloom.

"But it's pink!"

She shrugged and her grin broadened. "Sorry. It's the biggest robe I have. And you have really, um, broad shoulders."

Andie certainly knew how to get a guy into a flowered bathrobe. She thought I had broad shoulders! She pointed out the laundry room and I stepped in, taking off my wet clothes and tossing them into the dryer. I wrapped the robe around myself and pulled the sash tight. Just then I heard a tap on the window. Startled, I glanced up—and saw Jake's grinning face pressed against the glass.

Yow! I thought in dismay. *What's he doing here?*

But I'd hardly formed the question in my mind before I realized the answer. I'd mentioned this evening's plans to the guys at lunch that day. They knew we were here alone tonight, and they wanted to see what kind of action was going on.

I gulped, glancing desperately toward the kitchen. Any minute now, Andie could come in to see how I was doing. What if she spotted Jake? I made a "go away" motion with my hands, and Jake's face disappeared from the window.

I let out the breath I was holding. But my relief lasted only a second. Then Kyle's face appeared at the window. I groaned. This time I wasn't surprised when another face popped up beside Kyle's. Fuzzy.

Both of them were grinning like idiots. That's when it hit me—I was dressed in a robe. A *girl's* robe. Unless the guys decided I was a secret crossdresser, there was no doubt about what they were going to think.

I could run out and defend her honor, I thought, pulling the collar of the robe closed over my bare chest. *I could tell them the truth.*

I could do that. And they might believe me. Then again, probably not. So what was the point?

Either way, I decided, it could wait. If I ran out there now, Andie would find out what was going on. She would be hurt and angry. Why put her through that?

That's settled, then, I thought, biting my lip and wishing I could be certain I was doing the right thing. *I'll take care of it, but not right now. Later. And I'll make sure Andie never finds out.*

I gave the guys the finger, then pulled the curtain shut over their protesting waves. Smiling at the expressions of dismay on their curious faces, I hurried out of the laundry room.

Andie was waiting for me in the kitchen, two glasses of lemonade on the table. "I figured we could use a break before we get back to cleaning." She paused and frowned as a muffled crash came from outside. "Did you hear that? It sounds like someone's in the backyard."

I kept my expression calm. "I don't think so," I lied. I could picture Fuzzy tripping over a garbage can or grill out back. "It was probably just the dryer."

Andie looked uncertain. But she shrugged. "Okay," she said. "Come on, drink up. We've got a lot more work to do."

"Du-ude!" Fuzzy caught up to me outside of homeroom the next day. "You're the man." He grinned and raised his hand. I high-fived him automatically. "You'd better be careful, though. If you keep up this pace, you'll be too tired to come to school!"

I gulped, knowing that this was yet another chance to set the record straight. I was alone with Fuzzy. If I was ever going to challenge his story about Andie . . .

"Yo!" Jake jogged up to us. "What's up, guys?"

"Parker was just about to fill me in on his hot date with Andie last night," Fuzzy said. "So how about it, dude? Aren't you going to give us the four-one-one?"

I sighed, suddenly sick of how immature they were acting. "Yeah," I said, rolling my eyes. "You'll be reading all about it on the Internet."

"Hey, that's awesome. WWW dot I scored dot com!" Jake laughed, obviously missing my sarcasm.

This was getting out of hand. If I'd just told the truth about my friendship with Andie from the start . . . but there was no point in thinking about that now. I just had to figure out what to do next.

Just then Wendell Owen wandered past, intently focused on his biology textbook as he walked. Fuzzy stuck out his leg. Wendell never had a chance. His arms waving wildly, books flying everywhere, he did a belly flop onto the hard tile floor.

"Oops, you shouldn't read and walk at the same time," Jake said with a laugh.

For a moment Wendell just lay there. Then he rolled over onto his back, touching his glasses to make sure they were okay. They were fine, but a sticky yellow mess was oozing out of the pocket of his polyester shirt. Wendell junior.

Jake and Fuzzy laughed. "Bummer!" Jake said as the bell rang, signaling that it was time for us all to head to homeroom. "Marissa's not going to be happy with hubby today." He and Fuzzy walked away, still chuckling.

When they were gone, I helped Wendell up. "Sorry about your egg."

"Yeah." Wendell looked more resigned than unhappy. "I'm going to lose points for sure."

"You could substitute another egg," I suggested.

Wendell shook his head, shooting me a surprised look. "That would be cheating." He walked away toward his homeroom, leaving me to wonder if I could learn something from him. Like how to be honest.

Then I shook it off. The only lesson to be learned from Wendell was what would happen to me if I messed things up with Jake and the guys. There was no way I was ever going back to being a social outcast like Wendell Owen again.

Andie and I met at her locker after school. We had agreed to take care of the "dating" part of our assignment that evening after she finished her shift at the library.

"Hi," she greeted me when I arrived, glancing up from stacking her books neatly on the locker shelf. "Did you come up with any brilliant ideas for our big date?"

"Just one," I said, trying to sound as if I hadn't spent practically every second all day thinking about it. Which I had, of course. "I thought maybe we could go to the basketball game tonight. Support the home team *and* get credit."

"The basketball game?" She frowned. "I don't think that's such a good idea."

"Why not?"

She fished our egg out of her purse and held it up. "Well, for one thing, it wouldn't be good for the little one. All that noise, the crowds . . ."

I could tell that wasn't really the reason she didn't want to go to the game. *Maybe she's ashamed to go because half the team has seen her naked,* an evil little voice inside of me piped up.

On the other hand, maybe she wants to stay away from noise and crowds because she'd rather we go someplace nice and quiet and very, very private. . . .

"Stop it!" I said aloud, clapping my hands to my ears. Seeing that Andie was looking at me strangely—and who could blame her?—I smiled weakly. "Uh, I mean, you convinced me. So what should we do instead?"

She shrugged. "Dinner and a movie?"

"Okay." My heart skipped a beat. Dinner and a movie. The classic date. Suddenly this evening was starting to feel even less like a school assignment and more like real life. "But family films only, right?" I joked, to cover up what I was thinking. "After all, Junior's at that impressionable age."

Andie smiled.

"I'll meet you at Moe's at six, okay?"

She hesitated, then nodded. "Okay."

When I arrived at Moe's promptly at six o'clock, Andie was waiting for me just inside the door. I almost didn't recognize her for a second. Instead of the jeans and wool sweaters she usually wore to school, she had on a pale green dress that skimmed her body and made her skin sort of glow. And its short sleeves, scooped neck, and above-the-knee skirt let me see a whole lot more of that skin than I'd ever seen before.

I gulped, feeling color rise to my cheeks as I took it all in. A matching sweater was over her arm, along with her coat. Her blond hair was pulled back in a pair of sparkly butterfly clips, and she'd applied some kind of glossy stuff to her lips that made them shine. I couldn't take my eyes off her. I'd always thought she was beautiful, but tonight she took my breath away.

"Wow," I said, clearing my throat nervously. The old nerd inside of me was threatening to break out and start giggling uncontrollably at the whole concept that I—dorky Andrew Jackson Parker, lifelong social loser—was actually standing here with this incredible creature. "Uh, you look great."

"Thanks." Andie blushed. "Hey, I'm starved. Let's find a table."

We found a seat in a booth along the back wall. After the waitress took our order, we just sat there for a minute or two. I kept shooting looks at her across the table, trying not to seem like I was staring. She seemed a little uncomfortable. She kept playing with her napkin and clearing her throat.

But after a few minutes, the awkwardness mysteriously passed. I managed to stop obsessing over how gorgeous Andie looked—well, mostly, anyway—and we started talking the way we usually did. We started off with our project, then moved on to her job at the library, and then hit other topics, like history and school and life in general. Somewhere along the way our food arrived, and I guess I ate mine. But I had no idea what I was eating. All I could think about was our conversation.

We continued to talk long after our burgers— or whatever—were gone, moving effortlessly from one topic to another and then another. I felt as though I could talk to Andie forever and never run out of things to say. It was a nice feeling, especially since I'd never really experienced anything like it before. I wanted to tell her *everything* about myself, and wanted to know *everything* about her. But that's how it was with Andie. Don't get me wrong—I didn't 'fess up to my previous life as a nerd, but I sort of felt I could have. That she would have understood.

We were polishing off the last bit of a shared ice cream sundae and discussing all the places we wanted to visit in Europe when I noticed that a slightly overweight kid I vaguely recognized from my English class was walking up to our table. Andie smiled when she saw him. "Hi, Jeremy," she said with a smile.

"Hey, Andie," he replied. He shifted from foot to foot. "Listen, I'm really sorry to bother you. But I was just wondering—did you get the history assignment today? I forgot to write it down."

Andie chuckled. "So what else is new?" she said teasingly.

Jeremy shrugged and grinned. "Hey, at least I can always count on you to fill me in, right?"

I didn't much like the way he was looking at her. How well did Andie and this Jeremy kid know each other? Were they friends? More than friends? Had he kissed her, touched her, done more?

81

As Andie told him their homework assignment, I found myself digging my fingers into my knees under the table, so hard that I was sure I was leaving marks.

"So," I said when Jeremy had gone back to his own table, "he seemed nice. Is he a good friend of yours?"

Andie dipped her spoon into the sundae glass to scoop out one last bit of chocolate syrup. "Jeremy's a sweet guy," she said. "We sit next to each other in history class. Sorry, I guess I should have introduced you. I keep forgetting how new you are—you already fit in so well."

I was flattered enough that I couldn't bring myself to say anything else about Jeremy. But I couldn't stop thinking about him. Him and all the other guys. I found myself forming a vivid, full-color mental image of Fuzzy's big, beefy arms wrapped around Andie as he . . . and of Brent Carver from my gym class, bending down to kiss her all over her face before he . . .

I shook my head, trying to shake the images right out. This was driving me crazy. I had to know whether Andie was really the way the guys said she was. Whether the stories were true.

I glanced across the table at Andie, who was dabbing at her mouth with a napkin. Most of her shiny lip gloss was gone, but she still looked amazing.

Would it matter to me if the stories were true? Would I still want to hang out with her?

I barely had to think about that. Of course I would. I'd only known her for eight days, nine hours, and, oh, about seventeen minutes. But already I couldn't imagine my life without her.

But that was all the more reason to find out the truth, I reasoned. After all, I should know whether I had a shot at spending time with her after the marriage project was over, or whether the fact that she hadn't jumped my bones—the way she had, maybe, with all those other guys—meant that she just wasn't interested in a nerd like me.

I cleared my throat, trying to figure out how to ask what I wanted to ask without upsetting her. But before I could open my mouth, I heard a commotion up by the restaurant's entrance. Glancing over, I saw that Jake and the gang had just walked in.

"Hey," I commented, nodding toward them. "Looks like the basketball game is over."

"Looks that way," Andie replied, her voice and manner suddenly much more subdued than they had been. She reached for her sweater and slipped it on, pulling it closed across her chest.

I glanced over at my friends again. The guys had changed out of their basketball uniforms, but Lauren and Veronica and Courtney were still wearing their cheerleading uniforms. Fuzzy and Kyle were goofing around, punching each other and laughing. In fact, the whole group seemed to be in high spirits, which I took to mean that they must have won their game.

As they descended on a booth across the way, Jake spotted me and waved. Then he headed toward our table. His "wife," Veronica Morita, noticed his departure and followed, a slight frown on her pretty face.

"Yo," Jake greeted me. "What are you two up to?"

Before Andie or I could answer, Veronica grabbed Jake by the arm. "Hey," she said, sounding peeved. "Where do you think you're going? You said if we came here, we'd spend some quality time working on that stupid budget. We haven't even started it yet, you know. And you're nuts if you think I'm going to do it all this weekend while you're goofing off with your friends."

Jake rolled his eyes. "Nag, nag, nag," he said lightly. He glanced at Veronica. "Listen, why don't you go spend some quality time with yourself? I need to talk to my buddy Andy here."

Veronica glared at him. "Fine," she said icily. "But you're baby-sitting for the rest of the night." She pulled their egg out of her jacket pocket and tossed it to him.

"Whoa! Oh, no!" Jake fumbled the catch, sending the egg flying off to one side. He reached to grab it, but it slipped out of his grasp again and almost hit the table before he scooped it up. It wasn't until he grinned and said, "Psych!" that I realized he'd faked the whole thing.

Veronica rolled her eyes and left, heading back to her friends. I shook my head ruefully. "You'd better watch it, man," I told Jake. "I don't think Veronica's going to be too happy with you if you break Jake junior."

Jake tossed his egg in the air and caught it again. "No problem. I boiled the little sucker."

Just then the little bell over the entrance rang. Glancing over, I saw that Marissa had just come in.

Jake saw her too. He quickly pocketed the egg and straightened up. "Hey, listen, I've got to go. If wifey comes looking for me, tell her I'm in the john."

I watched as he hurried toward Marissa, intercepting her near the door. She looked wary at his approach, but in a matter of seconds his arm was around her and she was leaning into him, running one hand up his back beneath his jacket.

"Uh-oh," I said with a smile as Jake steered her back out the door. "Looks like someone's marriage is in some serious trouble."

Andie just rolled her eyes. She didn't smile at my joke. "We'd better get going," she said. "The movie starts soon, and we don't want to miss the previews."

"Uh, okay." I glanced at my watch. We still had twenty minutes before show time, and the movie theater was only a couple of blocks away. But I wasn't going to argue. "Let me just get the check."

I was pocketing my change after paying at the register when Fuzzy and Kyle got up from their table and came over. "Yo, Parker," Fuzzy said, glancing at Andie—or, more accurately, at Andie's legs—with an appreciative smile. "Where'd Jake go?"

"Uh, I'm not sure," I lied.

I noticed that Kyle was staring at Andie's legs too. "Well, at least we know he didn't sneak off to the alley to boink your wife, since she's still here."

Andie gasped and turned away, almost as if she'd been slapped. I felt a rush of rage toward Kyle and Fuzzy, stronger than any emotion I'd ever felt before. How dare they make her feel so awful? No matter what she'd done, she didn't deserve that.

"Lay off, man," I said hotly, clenching my fists at my sides and taking a step toward Kyle. "That was a totally harsh thing to say."

"What's with you?" Kyle asked, looking confused. "I was just goofing with you."

"Well, I don't think it's funny," I shot back. "In fact, I think you owe Andie an apology."

Kyle looked annoyed, and for a second I thought he might take a swing at me. Meanwhile, Fuzzy just shot me a curious glance before returning his full attention to Andie's legs.

Suddenly Kyle's face cleared. "Oh," he said. "Right. Sorry about that, man." He reached out and punched me lightly on the shoulder. Then he glanced at Andie. "Sorry. Guess that was pretty, uh, rude."

Andie shrugged without meeting his eyes. I put

one arm around her shoulders, feeling protective. "Come on," I said. "We should get going."

She nodded, her eyes downcast and her cheeks red. "Give me a second, okay? I just want to stop in the rest room."

"Okay." I squeezed her shoulders once and then released her. She hurried toward the rest rooms in the back of the restaurant.

When I turned back toward the guys, I found both of them grinning at me. "You're a pretty smart dude, Parker," Fuzzy commented.

"What?"

"He's right," Kyle said. "That was a really sharp move, playing the protective hero like that. That'll definitely keep her coming back for more."

"Huh?" I wasn't sure what he was talking about.

Fuzzy slung one big arm over my shoulders. "Yeah, we don't mind playing along—on one condition." He leered at me and winked suggestively. "You just have to promise to share all the gory details. We compare notes, you know? I mean, Andie's been a busy girl since she and I last did the deed. I'm wondering if she's, like, learned any interesting new tricks."

I shoved Fuzzy's arm away with another surge of anger. I was ready to let them have it—to tell them exactly what I thought of their stupid comments. To tell them that Andie and I hadn't done anything except kiss. To say that I knew what she was really like, and there was no way she could be the kind of girl they claimed she was.

But just then I spotted Andie coming back from the bathroom. As she walked past the booth where Jeremy was sitting with some friends, she paused and leaned over the table to say something to him. Even from across the room, I caught Jeremy's gaze wandering south of her face, and I remembered that low-cut neckline on her dress . . . .

My face flushed, and I couldn't speak. What did I know, anyway? What made me think I knew the truth about anything—including Andie?

Seven

FRIDAY NIGHT AT five minutes to six, the doorbell rang and I took a last look around our
house. It wasn't something I liked to admit, but I'd
never had a girl over to dinner before. Luckily, my
parents were taking it all in stride.

I hurried toward the front door, taking a deep
breath and barely surviving a moment of panic
when I tried to remember whether I'd brushed my
teeth. Sucking in more air, I tasted mint. I opened
the door. Andie was bundled up in a long wool
coat, her cheeks pink from the cold. She looked
adorable. "Wow, you live in a really great neighborhood," she said. "This house is amazing."

"Thanks." I was glad to see that she was in a
good mood. Tonight was her night to meet the in-
laws, and I really wanted things to go well.

She stepped inside and unwound her scarf. "I'm
pretty nervous about meeting your parents," she

said. "Imagine if we were a real couple! I'd be a basket case."

If we were a real couple. I felt a sort of stab somewhere in the area of my gut, but I shook it off. Of course we weren't a couple. It was all make-believe— just a school project. Still, I remained a little distracted by her words as I led her to the living room and introduced her to my parents.

"It's so great to meet you," Andie said, shaking their hands in turn. "A.J. has told me a lot about you."

"Yes, we're very proud of our *A.J.*" My mom's eyes twinkled as she shot me an amused glance. My face burned as I realized I'd neglected to mention my new nickname to them.

Dad didn't seem to have noticed. "So, Andie," he said jovially, rubbing his salt-and-pepper beard as he took his seat again in his favorite leather chair. "My son tells me you're interested in the social sciences, just like me."

Which of course led Andie to ask my father all about his job. That conversation lasted well into dinner before switching over to a more general discussion of the joys of travel. By the time we finished dessert and moved back into the living room, my parents were telling Andie about the summer when I was five and our whole family had gone to the Grand Canyon on vacation.

"Just a second." Mom stood and hurried toward the tall oak cabinet in the corner of the room. "I think we have some pictures of Andy riding a burro in the family albums." She opened the door and pulled out several leather-bound volumes.

My heart stopped. Literally. I had no problem with Andie seeing me on the burro. But there were plenty of other photos in those albums that I most definitely did not want her to see. Pictures of me posing with the chess club or holding up the city trophy I'd helped win as a charter member of the Science Whiz Quiz Team in seventh grade. A newspaper article about me winning the district spelling bee three years in a row.

In other words, a comprehensive visual history of my former life as a geek, in shiny bright Kodachrome.

I jumped to my feet. "Mom, you've got to be kidding. Andie doesn't want to look at those boring old photo albums."

"Of course I do," Andie said.

Mom shot me a puzzled look. "Yes, come on, sweetie. At least let her see this one. It's adorable, whether you admit it or not."

She pulled one album out of the stack she was holding. I recognized it with relief. It was the one that covered my first six years of life—before I started school and discovered my true identity as a nerd.

"Well, all right," I said. "But just that one. Then Andie and I really have to get some work done on our project."

Mom sat down on the couch beside Andie and they started paging through the book. Andie giggled at my baby pictures, especially one taken at age three, when I'd been fitted for my first pair of glasses. "You look adorable!" she exclaimed, glancing at me, her eyes sparkling. "I didn't know you wore glasses."

I shrugged. "Contact lenses," I mumbled. "Look, you don't have to pretend to be interested in those stupid old pictures."

Andie brushed back her long hair and studied the photos. "No, this is great," she said thoughtfully. "Actually, I was just thinking that we could use a baby picture of you and one of me in our project. We could scan them in and design a cool cover for the final report. It would be cute."

I quickly agreed and picked out a baby photo of myself that wasn't too embarrassing.

"I'll go scan it in right now," I volunteered quickly. Grabbing the pile of photo albums, which Mom had dropped on the coffee table—dangerously close to where Andie was sitting on the couch—I raced out of the room. Upstairs, I shoved the albums under my bed before heading to my computer and scanning in the photo.

When I came back downstairs, I discovered that Dad had dragged Andie out to his office to show her his artifacts. Mom was waiting for me in the living room. "Andie seems like a very nice girl," she said with a smile. "And I think she really likes you."

I blushed. It felt weird to be discussing the girl I liked with my mom. That had never happened before. I had never mentioned Amber to either of my parents. Thank goodness.

But I wasn't really thinking about Amber just then. I was only thinking about Andie. "Uh, whatever," I told Mom with a sheepish grin. "I'd better go rescue her from Dad before he starts trying to make her drink that canned yak's milk he brought back from wherever."

A few hours later, Andie finally insisted that she had to get home. My parents seemed reluctant to let her go, and so was I.

I walked her to the door. "I really like your parents," she said softly as she pulled on her coat. "Thank you for inviting me over to meet them."

"Sure." I didn't bother to remind her that it was all part of our project. Because suddenly it didn't feel much like a school assignment anymore.

I definitely liked the feeling.

The next morning in the student parking lot, I made the mistake of mentioning the previous evening to Jake when I ran into him. I guess I was still floating somewhere up north of cloud nine, because I also sighed and said, "Andie is great. She's really nice."

Jake punched me in the arm. "If that's what you want to call it." He chuckled wickedly.

I frowned. "No, I mean it," I protested. "We had a great time last night."

Jake looked at me carefully. "Hey, don't tell me you're really falling for her. I'm your friend, man, and I don't want to see you hurt. So take it from me. Andie isn't the kind of girl you want to go and fall in love with."

"You don't know her like I do."

He studied me with narrowed eyes. "No, I don't. But I don't want you breaking your heart over a girl who's not worth it."

I glared at him angrily. "You don't know what you're talking about."

"Look." Jake was more serious than I'd ever seen him. "I like you, Parker. You're a good guy. But I'm not sure you know what you're getting into with Andie Foster. I mean, it's one thing if you're just pulling this nice-boy crap because you want to keep getting laid." I guess he saw the look on my face when he said that, because he held up his hands appeasingly. "Not that I'm saying that's the case, dude. I'll take you at your word if you say you two never did the horizontal tango."

"I *respect* Andie," I said firmly. I didn't care anymore about looking cool in front of him. If he couldn't handle the fact that I cared about Andie as a person, not just a sex object, then that was his problem.

"That's what I'm trying to say here, dude." Jake's handsome face was worried. "You're obviously falling for this girl. You're, like, blinded by love or whatever. And that's what worries me." He shrugged. I guess the stubborn look on my face convinced him that his arguments were hopeless. "Anyway, I'm not going to say anything else about

Andie Foster—except that Fuzzy has never lied to me in his life. And he told me all about his nights with her. Look, man, we all saw you wearing her robe in her house. If you're not into divulging details, that's cool."

I just shook my head and headed into the school, leaving Jake to lock up his car. I didn't want him to see it, but his words had really made me think. Jake was my friend. I believed that. I also believed that he really thought Fuzzy was telling the truth.

But Fuzzy totally made up that stuff about sleeping with Andie, I thought. *He's just blowing smoke. She's not like that.*

But deep down inside, I wasn't quite as confident as I wished I could be. Did I really know Andie Foster as well as I thought I did?

Eight

SATURDAY NIGHT. DATE night.

You got that right, dude, Jake's voice said in my head. *And it could be your big night too!*

I winced. Jake hadn't actually said those words, at least not exactly. But earlier that day he and Kyle had stopped by to see if I wanted to shoot some hoops with them. When they'd heard my plans—dinner at Andie's house—they'd definitely perked up their ears with interest.

I did my best to put all that out of my head as Andie opened the door. She was wearing a blue shirt that matched the shade of her eyes, making them sort of glow. There was a smudge of something that looked like flour on her cheek, which made her look even cuter.

"Hi," I said, suddenly feeling a little choked up. Maybe this project was just a class assignment, but at the moment, at least, it felt so real it was spooky.

I sort of flashed forward, imagining that it was ten years down the road. That I was coming home from a long business trip or something. Maybe even a field project like my dad always did.

And that Andie was waiting for me at home. Looking just as glad to see me as she did right now, with a smudge of flour on her cheek and a familiar sparkle in her eye that only she had.

Feeling a little dizzy, I held out my hand. "Here," I said, stumbling over the words. "Uh, I brought flowers. For you."

"Thanks." Andie took the flowers and then stepped back to let me in. "They're beautiful. Come on in. Dinner's almost ready. How's the baby?"

I followed her into the kitchen, which smelled fantastic. That helped chase away my weird futuristic feelings. Taking our egg out of my pocket, I carefully set the box on the counter. "I spent all day wearing him out," I joked. "I'm hoping he's so tired he'll nap all evening."

I blushed as I suddenly realized what my words might sound like. Would Andie think I was expecting anything in particular to happen tonight?

I decided the best thing to do was change the subject—fast. "Actually, though, I was afraid he might get squashed before I made it over here. I was hanging out with the guys this afternoon, and Fuzzy almost sat on him a couple of times. Even Junior's box wouldn't protect him from that!"

Andie chuckled, but it sounded a little forced. "Sounds typical," she said. "Fuzzy always acts before he thinks." She shook her head and sighed. "Let me tell you, I'm really glad I got you as a partner for this project instead of someone like Kyle or Fuzzy. I'm sorry, I know they're your friends, but sometimes they can be really immature."

That was the perfect chance for me to bring up her reputation—to ask her to tell me the real story. But I couldn't do it. I didn't want to mess up our evening before it even got started. Besides, what if she admitted it was true? What would I do then?

I shrugged and grinned weakly, feeling like the world's biggest coward. "The guys are okay," I said. "They just like to goof around, you know?"

"Whatever." She didn't sound mad, just resigned. "Why don't we do our journal entry? The food will be ready in a few minutes."

We filled out a page or two in our project diary, falling back into the comfortable pattern of joking around about Junior and talking about the assignment. Soon after that was finished, we sat down to eat. We even toasted our partnership in the project with ginger ale served up in wineglasses.

I was feeling almost as giddy as if there had been real wine in those glasses. "I'm really glad we're working together," I told Andie earnestly. "I've— I've really enjoyed it."

She smiled shyly. "Me too," she admitted, her voice soft and tentative. "I was kind of worried in the beginning."

"Why?"

She played with her food, not meeting my eyes

directly. "I noticed you when you first came to Fairview. I kind of hoped— Well, but then I saw you hanging out with Jake and Fuzzy and all those guys. So I figured you were just like them."

I protested that, of course. But I sort of understood why she might feel that way. People tended to hang around with people who were a lot like them. That was why the jocks formed one group, and the musicians and other artsy types hung in another, and the geeks had yet another. It was the way of the world, at least in high school.

And for once I was in the right crowd. But it had given Andie the wrong idea. "Listen," I said, leaning forward until my shirt was practically pressing against my meat loaf. But at last she looked up at me. "Jake and Fuzzy and those guys don't matter. What matters is you and me. And I—I really like you, Andie." I couldn't believe I was saying this, but I plunged onward. "And I don't just mean because of the project. I don't just mean as a friend. I—"

Before I could go on, she sort of cried out, stopping me short. "Please," she said. "Before you say anything else, I need to know. My reputation—I mean, I know you must have heard the stories. Or read some of the horrible things guys have written about me on the bathroom walls."

I could feel my face turning beet red. "Uh, I . . ."

Her shoulders slumped and she kept her gaze on her plate. "Once all those awful rumors started about what a nympho I was, that was that. No matter how much I denied the stories, no one believed me. And since I was new in town, it was really just me against everyone else."

"What happened?" I asked tentatively. "How did the rumors begin?" I didn't want her to think I doubted her word. But I had to know.

Andie looked at me for a long moment, chewing her lower lip. I guessed she was wondering if she could trust me. Then, finally, she pushed her plate away and took a deep breath. And the words began to tumble out of her.

"Mom and I moved to Fairview at the end of last August," she began. "I was worried about the move—I'd been at my old school since kindergarten, so I'd never had to make new friends before. I wasn't sure I'd be any good at it." She shrugged. "Anyway, the first week was tough. All the kids here knew each other already, and nobody really seemed too interested in me." She cleared her throat. "Except for Fuzzy. He sat next to me in English class, and we started joking around a little—you know, like him begging me to fill him in on each day's reading assignment because he'd blown it off. Me giving him a hard time about forgetting how to read." She smiled sort of wistfully, as if gazing through a window at a happier, simpler past. Which, in a way, I guess she was. "And when he found out I worked at the library, he asked if I'd help him out with the research paper we'd just been assigned."

I nodded. That sounded like Fuzzy. "Then what happened?"

"What happened was I made the mistake of saying yes. Fuzzy was really great at first. He introduced me to some of his friends, and he and I spent, like, three days together after school, first at the library and then over at his house, working on the outline for his paper."

I winced. I could already guess what was coming. But I didn't say a word. She was staring at her hands, which were folded in her lap.

"On the third day," she said quietly, "I was getting ready to take off. That was when Fuzzy decided to make a move on me. I stopped him—I didn't like him that way. I told him I just wanted to be friends. But I guess he couldn't handle the rejection." She frowned. "He stopped talking to me."

"Bummer," I said quietly. As much as I liked Fuzzy, I could totally believe what she'd just said. Fuzzy was used to getting his way, especially when it came to girls. He wouldn't want it to get out that he'd been shot down.

Andie took another deep breath. "You know that guy Steven Stockwell?" She glanced over at me and I nodded, vaguely recalling a short, stocky guy from my chemistry class. "He and Fuzzy are on the football team together," she went on. "Steven was one of the people Fuzzy introduced me to. Well, a few days after the, um, incident with Fuzzy, Steven asked me out. And I was stupid enough to think it was because he was actually interested in me. As a person."

I could hear the raw pain in her voice. "Listen,

you don't have to finish the story," I began.

But she shook her head sharply and went on. "Steven and I went out maybe three or four times." Andie twirled a strand of her blond hair around her finger. "I was sort of psyched about it, actually, even though I knew by halfway through the first date that there wasn't really any chemistry between us. In my old hometown, guys and girls mostly went out in groups. They didn't date the way kids do here. So it was all new to me, you know?" She sighed and her expression turned bitter. "And I guess I just didn't know the rules. After I let Steven down gently—we never even kissed, by the way—I remembered his friend Frank. I'd met him when Steven and I went bowling one time. We'd had a good time goofing around, so I called Frank and asked if he wanted to go bowling again sometime." She stopped for a moment and stared at her hands again. "When he said yes, I actually started to feel *popular*. I just never thought what it would look like. First hanging out with Fuzzy, then his friend Steven, then Frank. All within about two weeks."

"But a lot of girls date different guys," I protested. "That's no crime."

"I know." Andie sounded almost angry. "But what I didn't know at the time was that Fuzzy had already told the whole world he'd scored with me. That's why Steven kept asking me out, even though he knew as well as I did that we were never going to be an item. And that's why Frank got mad and called me a tease when I wouldn't put out after our first date. He said I'd do it with every other guy in town, so why not him? That's when I started to realize what was going on."

I could hardly believe what she was saying. It seemed like something out of a bad movie from the fifties. But looking into her face, I knew that I had to believe it. "I'm sorry," I murmured, not knowing what else to say.

Andie shrugged. "Ever since then, it's been more of the same," she said quietly. "At first I tried to just ride it out. I even figured that if I went out with a few more guys, they'd see what I was really like and people would know the truth." She laughed shortly. "Bad move. No guy wanted to admit that he was the only one who couldn't get lucky with me. So they all pretended they'd bagged me. The stories just got worse and worse."

I felt horrible. Andie looked so sad that I wanted to do something—anything—to wipe that hurt, haunted, lonely expression off her face. But I just sat there, feeling helpless. "Does your mother know about this?" I asked after a moment.

"No way." Andie shuddered. "She had enough on her mind, starting a new job and all the rest. Besides, what could she do? The damage was already done."

I took a deep breath. For once I wasn't going to be a coward. I walked around the table, sat down next to her, and took her hand. "I'm so sorry. I have to admit, I've heard a lot of . . . stories . . . about you. And at first I wasn't sure what to think. But I should have known better. I should have asked for your side of the story before this. I'm sorry."

She just stared at me for a moment, and I was afraid I'd said the wrong thing. Then, suddenly, she collapsed against me. "Thank you," she said, her voice muffled by my shirt. "It just feels so good to tell someone about this. To feel like I finally have a—a friend." Her voice broke on the last word.

I put my arms around her and patted her shoulder awkwardly. "I am your friend, Andie. Don't forget that. You can count on me."

She sniffed and sat up, wiping her eyes with one hand. "Thanks," she said thickly. "I just— Thanks."

I loosened my hold on her to give her a little space, but I didn't let go. Instead I raised my hand to her chin. She gazed at me with big blue eyes made even bigger and more luminous by her recent tears. Her lips were trembling slightly, and before I could think twice about what I was about to do, I covered her mouth with my own.

This time she didn't jump away. The moment stretched into a lot of moments. It was the best kiss I'd ever had. Not that I had a whole lot to compare it to. But it was better than anything I could have imagined, even in my wildest dreams.

Finally I realized I'd better come up for air before I passed out from sheer joy. I pulled away, keeping my arms wrapped around her. "That was nice," I whispered tenderly, stroking her chin with one finger.

"Really?" She gazed up at me, her blue eyes soft and vulnerable.

The moment froze between us and I opened my mouth to finish what I'd started to say before—that I wanted us to be much more than friends.

But then she cleared her throat and moved away, back to her own chair. "So," she said. "Now you know my whole life story. What about you? Do you have any scandalous stories to tell?"

I wasn't sure what to think. Hadn't she liked the kiss as much as I did? Was she disappointed? I couldn't really tell, since she was looking down at her plate again as she spoke, pushing her salad around with her fork.

I couldn't tell what she was thinking. But I knew what I was thinking. We'd really connected there for a few minutes. And not just with the kiss. Before that too, when she was sharing her past with me. Now, since Andie had told me about herself, I wanted to share the real Andrew Jackson Parker with her as well.

So I told her about my old life in Chicago. I told her about my plan to become popular. I even told her some other stuff—like the real reason I decided to change my life. I told her about Amber.

She didn't say much about that part of the story, though she nodded understandingly now and then. When I was finished, I guess I was feeling pretty vulnerable. I was half expecting her to stand up and say, *Amber was right. You're not good enough for me. Now pack up your pocket protector and get out.*

But she didn't say anything like that. She just nodded thoughtfully and stayed silent for a moment or two. "So Jake and those guys aren't really your friends?" she asked at last.

I hesitated, knowing what she wanted me to say. But I couldn't do it. "No, that's not really true," I said carefully. "I really do like Jake and all of them, especially now that I'm getting to know them better. They're fun to be around. And they're good guys once you get to know them. Sometimes they just don't think about, you know, other people."

"Like me." Andie's voice was bitter, but then she shook her head and smiled wryly. "Don't worry, I'm not mad about who your new friends are. It doesn't matter." She squeezed my hand. "Not anymore, now that I know I can trust you."

I felt a stab of guilt at her words. Could she trust me? True, I hadn't actually told anyone we were sleeping together. But I hadn't done as much as I could have to prevent them from jumping to all the wrong conclusions.

Then she leaned over to kiss me again, and I forgot all about that. For a very long time.

Nine

"DETAILS, PARKER, WE want details."
"Yeah, real up-close-and-personal details. Juicy ones," Kyle added with a leer as he and Jake sat down on either side of me in the cafeteria on Monday.

"How was your weekend? Did you and Marissa confess your affair to your wife yet?" I asked Jake jokingly, hoping to distract him from the topic of Andie and me. I'd managed to avoid the guys' questions all morning, but I knew I was running out of time. I had to tell them the truth about me and Andie. But it wasn't going to be easy.

Jake waved off my question without bothering to answer. That was when I knew my time had run out. "Come on, Parker," he said warningly. "We want words. Pronto."

I sighed, pushing away my tuna sandwich. Suddenly I didn't have much of an appetite. "I had dinner at Andie's house last night, as part of our assignment. End of story."

"Yeah, right." Jake rolled his eyes, looking a bit annoyed. "You two were alone all evening—you told us that yourself. You're telling me that you and the hottest girl in school had the house to yourself, and nothing happened?"

Kyle was staring at me curiously. "Hold up," he said. "I think I know what's going on here. Courtney kept yapping about Andie all weekend. Saying she talked to her and Andie claimed it was all lies. That she never got around with all those dudes."

Jake snorted. "Right. Tell that to Fuzzy. And the rest of the guys who bagged her." He pursed his lips and stared at me evenly. "Man, I can understand sticking up for her to make yourself look good. But she's not here now. If you don't start leveling with us soon, we may start thinking you're the only loser who couldn't land her." He smirked. "What happened, man? Did things get too hot and heavy for you?"

"Give me a break," I snapped before I could stop myself. "Real men don't have to sit around the cafeteria bragging about what they're doing. They just do it and keep their mouths shut."

Kyle let out a whoop, leaning across me and shoving Jake halfway off his seat. "Way to tell him, dude," he crowed, slapping me on the back.

I winced, and not only because Kyle didn't know his own strength. Obviously I'd given the guys the way wrong impression yet again. I glanced up and saw Fuzzy heading toward us with his lunch tray. I wished he would speak up and admit that he'd never been with Andie. That it was all lies.

Still, I knew I couldn't count on Fuzzy bailing me out. Clearly he'd decided that his own reputation as a stud was at stake, and that meant he was willing to ruin Andie's life. It didn't make me like him any better, but I could sympathize, sort of. After all, wasn't I guilty of the same kind of thing? Hadn't I let things get this far when just a few words could have cleared it up?

I swear to you all, I didn't sleep with Andie. And I'm not planning to—not anytime soon, anyway. I respect her too much. I love her.

That thought stunned me so much that I almost fell off my seat. I loved her. I was in love with her. Truly, madly, deeply. But as mind-blowing as that was, it didn't really help me with my dilemma. How could I convince my friends what Andie was really like without blowing everything that I'd worked so hard to accomplish at my new school?

As Fuzzy sat down and started ribbing Jake about his renewed romance with Marissa, I tried to come up with a plan. If I could just show my new friends the real Andie, maybe they would see for themselves that their ideas about her were all wrong. Maybe if Fuzzy got to know her again, he would feel guilty enough to confess that he'd made up that stuff about scoring with her. I knew that would be enough to convince Jake, and once Jake was on Andie's side, she was golden. Wasn't that how I'd wound up popular myself?

Just then Jake said something about taking Marissa to the Valentine's Day dance, and a little lightbulb went on in my brain. Of course! The dance was coming up at the end of next week. And I was already planning to ask Andie to go with me. Even if that alone wasn't enough to convince the guys that I was serious about her, I could make sure they spent some time with us once we got there. Then they would get to see the real Andie Foster instead of the false one scrawled on the bathroom walls.

Once I figured that out, I couldn't wait to ask her to the dance. I hoped to catch her at her locker right after school. Unfortunately, my chemistry teacher had other ideas. He kept me after class for what felt like an hour, raving about my brilliant performance on the quiz we'd taken on Friday and babbling about how I should go into science as a career someday. I listened, feeling both impatient at the delay and relieved at the timing. Just imagine if he'd said something like that in front of the whole class! My whole image as a cool, carefree jock type would have been blown in a big way.

Finally I was able to make my escape, after promising to look into summer youth courses at the university. I raced to Andie's locker, but she was already gone.

"Oh, well," I muttered, heading down the hall to my own locker. I would just have to catch up to her at the library.

I felt like running the whole way to campus, but the sidewalks were icy, and I wouldn't be able to do much dancing with my leg in a cast. So I took my time, which also gave me a few minutes to think.

The more I thought about what I was about to do, the more nervous I got. What if Andie said no? After all, she kept saying how much she wanted us to be friends. Wasn't that sometimes code for *Get lost, creep, I'd date King Kong before I'd be seen in public with you,* or something like that?

Just as my stomach was churning with anxiety, I remembered our kisses. I couldn't have been mistaken about what she was feeling then, could I? What she was saying by kissing me like that? She had kissed me as though she meant it.

But what if she kissed all the guys like that?

Stop it! I told myself angrily. *Those rumors aren't true. She told you so herself.*

I believed her. I really did. More to the point, I loved her. Being with her was more important than those stupid rumors, more important than anything that happened or didn't happen last semester. Maybe even more important than being popular.

I stopped short, almost skidding on a patch of ice. Was that true? Was being with Andie more important to me than being part of the in crowd?

Don't be a dork, Parker, I thought, getting my feet moving again. I was only a couple of blocks from the library now. *You don't have to choose. You can have it all. All you have to do is ask her to that dance, and the rest will practically take care of itself.*

111

I was in a good mood again as I burst into the reception area. Andie was sitting behind the desk shuffling some papers around. She glanced up when I entered. But instead of smiling at me, she frowned and crossed her arms over her chest. "What are you doing here?"

"I came to see you. I . . . I wanted to ask you something."

"You've already asked me a lot of questions, Andrew Jackson Parker. My mistake was thinking that you had listened to my answers."

I had no idea what she was talking about, but I suddenly noticed that her blue eyes were as cold as ice. "Wait, Andie. I wanted to ask . . ."

"Yes?"

I still didn't like the way she was looking at me, but I took a deep breath and plowed on, trying to focus on the plan. The plan that would make everything perfect. "I wanted to ask you, um, if you'll go to the Valentine's Day dance with me."

"I suppose you think I should be grateful that you asked me to the dance."

"Grateful?" I didn't understand.

"Wait here."

Andie left me speechless as she strode toward the staff room behind the desk. I wrinkled my forehead in confusion as I waited for her to return. What was going on? Why did she suddenly seem so mad at me?

A few seconds later Andie returned. In her hand she held Junior.

She took him out of his box and began tossing him back and forth in her hands. "Be careful," I couldn't help saying as Junior sailed through the air.

Andie narrowed her eyes. "What's the matter? Are you worried I might drop the egg?"

"I, well, I—" I gulped as she tossed it again, catching it just inches before it splattered on the desktop. I didn't understand what she was doing. We had to care for our egg for another twenty-four hours. We were supposed to deliver our oral reports the following day, Tuesday.

"The egg is fragile." She tossed Junior up again and caught him. "Just like trust is fragile. I trusted you."

"Andie, please. Put Junior down and tell me—"

"I ran into a couple of your friends after school today."

With a sinking feeling, I started to clue in to what this was all about. I'd tried to do the right thing, but not hard enough. Instead I'd let the guys think I'd scored with Andie. Again. "Er, what did they say?"

"Marissa said the news is all over school. You told everyone that I—that we—"

"No!" I interrupted desperately, holding up both hands as if to ward off the words before she could say them. "I mean it, Andie. I never said anything like that."

Her lips were a tight white line in her pale face. "But when they started telling their stories about me, you never said anything about us *not* sleeping together either, did you?" She paused, giving me a second to deny it.

When I didn't say anything, she nodded with grim satisfaction. "You let the guys think whatever they wanted because it made you look cool. A.J.— no, excuse me, *Andy* Parker is willing to do whatever is necessary to keep his friends. You're worse than the stupid jocks. They may be jerks, but at least it's sort of bearable because they lie out in the open. You changed your outside, Andy, but it's your inside that needs the real changing."

"Andie, no," I protested weakly. "That's not how it is."

"Isn't it? Then tell me that you corrected the guys. That you swore to them that nothing happened between us. That you told Fuzzy that you know he's a liar."

I opened my mouth and then shut it again. "Andie, I'm sorry. Please, just give me another chance! I have a plan—I mean, if we went to the dance together, I'm sure the guys would change their minds. You know, when they saw that you were with me."

As soon as the words were out of my mouth I knew I'd made a fatal mistake. Her blue eyes had turned sad and hurt, but now they were shooting fire again. "Oh, really? Everything will be okay because I'll be with Mr. Cool?" She glared at me. Very slowly and carefully she enunciated every word. "Andrew Jackson Parker, you are *not* cool."

I was so stunned that I couldn't reply. She started to stomp away but then turned back to me.

"Oh, I almost forgot." She held up Junior to give me a good look. Then she turned and rapped the egg against the hard surface of the library desk, cracking the shell. Before I could react, she lifted it over my head and split it open, dribbling gooey yolk and slimy white all over my face.

Definitely not cool.

Flip the book over for Andie's side— and find out how their story ends!

Don't miss any of the books in *Love Stories*
—the romantic series from Bantam Books!

Andie's Side

One

"MS. FOSTER," MS. Church said, checking her list, "your partner for egg week will be Mr. Parker."

I could hardly believe my ears. *Wow,* I thought, feeling myself starting to blush. *Could my luck at Fairview High finally be changing?*

"Hey, I don't blame you for being stunned, man," Jake Wilkins's loud, obnoxious voice called out from the back of the room. "You got matched with the famous Andie Foster!"

No. Apparently my luck hadn't changed that much.

I ducked my head as the rest of the class cracked up, barely looking up long enough to see Ms. Church hand our egg to Andy Parker. For a second I wished she'd given it to me instead, so I could have whirled and flung it at Jake. Or maybe at his buddy Fuzzy—right between the eyes, splattered all over his fat, lying face.

1

I sighed, wishing for the millionth time that my life could be normal again. But wishing never seemed to work. And I couldn't figure out how else to make it happen, short of running away from home and enrolling myself in a different school, where no one knew me. Or my reputation.

Of course, that really wasn't an option. Mom had a good job here in Fairview—the best one she'd ever had. For the first time, she got to manage a whole department at the store. Her boss respected her, other people looked up to her. So what if she had to work long hours? I could tell that she loved it.

Besides, I thought, *I love my job here too. So maybe there are one or two other reasons to stay in Fairview.* I turned to glance at Andy Parker again. I wasn't sure why I found him so . . . interesting. But I'd noticed him the first day he walked into psych class the week before.

Maybe it was partly his looks—he was tall, with broad shoulders and nice dark hair. But there was something more too. Something in his face, his expression, that made me think—or at least *hope*—that he might be the one guy who would understand.

"Way to go, man," Jake said in a stage whisper that could have carried all the way to Canada.

I felt myself freeze. It was still a shock every time. I should've been used to it. It had been going on for months now. But I guess a part of me still just didn't believe they could really be talking about me.

But Jake's comment wasn't the worst part. Andy turned toward Jake with a grin—a pleased and

confident grin that told me he'd heard the stories about me and planned to make the most of our partnership.

So much for Mr. Different and Understanding, I thought bitterly. *I should have known. After all, it was obvious that he fit right in with Jake's group from his very first day. That means he's one of them. The enemy.*

Feeling sad and angry at the same time, I hunched down in my seat, fixed my gaze on my own desk, and stayed like that for the rest of the period.

After the bell rang, Andy came over to talk about the project. The conversation didn't go too well at first. I was so busy trying not to yell at him—*How could you believe them? You don't even know me! It's not fair!*—that I could barely manage to spit out rational replies to his comments.

"Maybe we could meet up after school," he said.

Yeah, right. I could just imagine what he was thinking: *The sooner we get together, the sooner Andie Foster can start making all my nasty dreams come true.*

I wasn't about to make it easier for him to daydream about that. "I work at the university library after school," I said bluntly. "We'll have to make it later."

"You work at the university library? Cool!"

I glanced at him suspiciously. His whole face had lit up, and I could tell he wasn't faking. He actually thought it was cool that I worked at the library! Weird. I didn't think Jake or most of his friends even knew what a library was.

3

"Yeah," I said cautiously, suddenly feeling a tiny flare of hope. Maybe he wasn't like them after all. Maybe I should give him a chance. "I work in the history wing."

We set up a time to meet. I was so busy thinking about Andy and all my different, conflicting impressions of him, that it wasn't until I was sitting in English class fifteen minutes later that I realized I hadn't even remembered that one of us had to take care of the egg all day. Since I hadn't taken it, that meant Andy had the first shift.

Oh, well, I thought with a smile, ducking my head so nobody would see my expression. *I guess this will be a test. If he doesn't break little Eggbert by the time we meet tonight, maybe I'll give him a chance.*

I guess I was nervous about my first meeting with Andy, because I was like a whirling dervish that afternoon at the library. I managed to shelve an hour's worth of books in about twenty minutes, and I typed up a whole week's worth of late notices. That took a little longer, though. I kept accidentally typing "Andy" instead of whatever the name was supposed to be, and having to back up and delete it.

As seven-thirty loomed closer, I started getting nervous. Maybe it was because I hadn't hung out with a guy alone since the previous fall. After that last "date" back in early November, when some senior guy started groping me before we'd even made it off my front porch, I hadn't exactly been eager to give it another try.

Don't be a fool, I told myself as I wandered toward

4

the front reception area. *This isn't a date. It's a school project. All you have to do is make it clear that it's all business.*

I told my boss I was through for the day, then checked my watch. It was still only seven-twenty, so I grabbed a big illustrated history of the Middle Ages off the shelving cart and hopped up onto the low returns desk to flip through it. Reading about other times and places always made me feel a little calmer—sometimes I could get so caught up in imagining the era I was reading about that I forgot myself and everything around me. I definitely needed that kind of distraction right then.

Hearing someone clear their throat behind me, I glanced up, realizing I'd become lost in an old color plate of a medieval village. Andy was standing there, just a few yards away. He was staring at me, that certain look in his eyes. The same look I'd seen in that senior's eyes just before he'd tried to stick his hands up my shirt right there in front of my own house.

I frowned, irrationally disappointed yet again. Obviously the library thing was a fluke. He was just like the others. "I'm almost finished," I muttered. "I'll get my bag and jacket."

Taking a few deep breaths as I hurried into the staff room to grab my stuff, I managed to calm down a little. *Business,* I told myself firmly. *Just act like this is only business. He'll get the hint. He'll have to.*

By the time I rejoined Andy a moment later, I was able to speak to him normally. I'd had a study hall that afternoon, so I'd done a little preliminary

work on our project, like coming up with a rough schedule for the week and starting on our budget. I guess I was feeling a little guilty about sticking him with the egg all day. First on my schedule was stopping by the Shop 'n' Save to fill in some prices on the budget sheet. Andy seemed fine with that plan, so we headed over to the store.

As we walked, our hands shoved in our coat pockets against the sharp wind that was picking up now that the sun was down, he kept trying to make small talk. I really wasn't interested in chatting, but it was hard to resist some of his questions. Especially when he started asking about my job.

"How'd you land such a great job when you just moved here?" he queried at one point.

I glanced at him quickly, trying to remember if I'd mentioned that I was relatively new in town too. As far as I knew, I hadn't. That meant someone else had been telling Andy about me. And that had to be bad news. "They gave me a shot because I worked at the public library in my old hometown. How did you know I just moved here?"

He waved one hand casually. "I hear things."

He wasn't meeting my eyes when he said it. I frowned, feeling the same helplessness, humiliation, and rage that I always felt when I thought about my situation.

I tensed, waiting for what always came next: the first contact. Sometimes it was just a touch on the arm or the face. Other times the guy would slip an arm around my waist or take my hand as we

walked. The biggest jerks usually skipped that subtle stuff and went straight for the payoff, moving immediately to kissing and grabbing.

I always stopped it as soon as I realized what was happening. The first few times, I'd been naive enough to think that it was okay to let them get away with a little pleasant hugging and kissing. That those things could be enough, like they were for the guys I hung out with in my old hometown.

But not in Fairview. Now that I was a few months older and wiser, I knew what to expect from the beginning.

Andy surprised me, though. Instead of making his move, he changed the subject, asking me more about my job and even making me laugh by making a horrible face when he mentioned that he thought history was boring.

That threw me off balance. I found myself explaining why I found history so cool. And he really seemed to be listening too—listening and maybe even understanding. He also confessed that his full name was Andrew Jackson Parker.

That name didn't really fit him, and I told him so. "I'm not sure I see you as an Andy either," I added thoughtfully, looking him up and down. It was true. To me, the name Andy belonged on a little boy, or maybe an immature frat dude back at the college. The guy standing in front of me needed a friendlier name—more quirky and curious, more open and straightforward, like his gold-flecked brown eyes. . . .

Suddenly I realized that maybe it wasn't too polite

to tell someone their name didn't suit them. Also, I realized I'd been staring at Andy for a long moment. How long, I wasn't even sure. He was staring back, but I couldn't tell what he was thinking.

"Oh," I mumbled, blushing as I tore my gaze away. "I mean, well . . . Whatever. Look, there's the supermarket." I'd never been so glad to see the neon sign of the Shop 'n' Save in my life.

We headed into the store. I was still thinking about that moment outside, but I babbled about this and that to cover my confused feelings. What was Andy Parker doing to me, anyway? I knew what guys were like, what they always wanted from me. . . .

I decided to stop thinking about that. It wasn't like he was going to start sticking his tongue down my throat right there in the dairy aisle. Even Fuzzy Rywinski had more class than that.

It was actually pretty easy to relax and joke around with Andy. I kidded him about having to pitch in and be a liberated "husband," and he told a funny story about not being able to cook. We also got into a goofy discussion about eggs, which was pretty lame but still made me laugh.

We also talked a little more about our families. It seemed like Andy had a really nice one—his parents sounded smart and interesting and generally pretty cool.

Meanwhile, of course, we were also making notes for our project. Naturally, one of the items on our budget was baby supplies. Okay, so maybe Eggbert wasn't a real baby. But I knew Ms. Church expected us to act as if he were.

We turned down the aisle with the diapers and stuff, and I started jotting down prices. I was just leaning over to read the price sign in front of some baby food when I heard someone bellowing Andy's name from nearby.

It was Jake. Just my luck.

He and Fuzzy were heading our way, goofy grins on their faces. I was so blown away by their sudden, unwelcome appearance that I hardly heard Jake's first moronic comment—something about me being "the little woman."

But I certainly couldn't miss what Fuzzy said next. "Hey, you two. Been getting lots of practice making babies?" Laughing like it was the wittiest thing anyone ever said, he started jumping around in front of me, acting like a total jerk.

I did my best to ignore him, though I could almost feel my face turning brighter and brighter red. Why did they have to come along and ruin things? Just when I was starting to convince myself that maybe I'd been right in the first place. Maybe Andy *was* different from the other guys.

Of course, he wasn't exactly leaping to my defense. He just stood there, looking back and forth from me to the guys with a totally blank expression.

"Yo, Andie," Jake said, leering at me and sort of leaning against the nearest display, trapping me between him and the shelf. "If you want to do a little extra-credit work for this marriage thing, just give me a call, okay?"

I shouldered my way out from under him and

scowled. But I wasn't about to dignify his comment with a reply, so I forced myself to turn away as Fuzzy burst out laughing.

"Yeah!" he snorted. "Good old Andie's a real dedicated student when she likes the subject."

Finally Andy spoke up. "Hey, guys," he interrupted, "we're trying to work here." He started to shoo them back to their own "wives," who must've been in some other part of the store. But before they went, Jake made one last comment—something about how I was "loose"—and I just lost it.

I couldn't take it for one more second. I knew I was about to burst into tears, and there was no way I was going to give those guys the satisfaction of seeing me cry. For a second I just stood there, trying to regain control. But it wasn't working. I turned and raced out of the store as fast as my feet would take me.

"Andie, wait up!" I heard Andy calling behind me.

Hearing his voice only made me run faster. To think I'd thought he was nice. What a sucker.

I guess I'm not much of a sprinter, because Andy caught up to me before I'd made it halfway across the parking lot. He grabbed me by the arm and started babbling about how he wasn't like those other guys.

Yeah, right.

"Look," he said. "Jake can be a jerk. No question about it. But you can't just assume I'm the same way because I hang out with him sometimes. That's not fair."

That brought me up short. Was I really being

unfair? Was I judging Andy without having all the facts—the same way most of the school had judged me last fall?

"Well . . ." I hesitated. Should I trust him? Or was I just setting myself up for more humiliation? I had no idea. But something about the way Andy was looking at me with those big puppy-dog brown eyes of his made me nod. "That's true," I said at last.

I wasn't sure if I was doing the right thing. But I decided to let him walk me home. As we walked and talked, I found myself relaxing again. At least a little. Somehow, being with him made me feel safe—that is, as long as his meathead friends weren't around.

I found myself thinking about his name again. He still didn't seem like an Andy to me. Besides, now that we were partners, the Andie/Andy thing just seemed too confusing.

That's when I came up with the perfect nick-name: A.J.

He seemed to like it too.

A.J. Perfect.

TWO

FOR ONCE, I wasn't dreading school when I arrived on Tuesday. I'd had a great dream about A.J. the night before. I didn't remember the details when I woke up. But I knew that I'd been in it too, and that it was good. It left me with a happy feeling.

That didn't last long. "Good morning, Andie," a haughty voice said from behind me as I twirled the lock on my locker.

I glanced over my shoulder and winced. It was Marissa Carpenter. Most of the girls at Fairview weren't too fond of me, but Marissa hated me even more than the rest. "Hello, Marissa," I said cautiously.

She stepped closer, giving me a whiff of her sweet, cloying perfume. "So you and the new guy seem to be hitting it off," she said. Her face was smiling, but her green eyes were icy. "What's up with that? Anything serious, or is he just your latest boy toy?"

The comment didn't deserve an answer, but the

way she was looking at me, I knew she was going to be a lot harder to ignore than the guys were. "Not that it's any of your business," I said coolly. "But if you ever paid attention in class, you'd know that Andy and I are psych partners." I almost slipped and called him A.J., but I caught myself just in time. No way did I want her to know that I'd given him a nickname.

She shrugged. "Glad to hear it," she cooed. "Because my friend Lauren thinks Andy's pretty cool, and she's sure he's going to ask her to the Valentine's dance. And I'd hate to see him get distracted by your . . . charms." Her gaze slithered down over me, and I had the urge to tug at my skirt to make it longer, or pull up the scoop neck on my sweater.

I hated that she made me feel so—so *dirty,* just by giving me a look. Inside I was fuming. But I did my best to sound calm as I answered. "You know how it is, Marissa," I said. "Sometimes when guys are bored with what they have, they start looking around for something better."

Her lips went white as she pressed them together, her green eyes spitting fire. "Slut!" she hissed.

After that brilliant comeback, she turned and stomped away. I smiled sadly, knowing I would pay for my comments. I remembered as well as she did how Jake had come on to me at the homecoming dance, grabbing me and trying to kiss me while Marissa was off in the bathroom. I'd done nothing to invite it, and I'd pushed him away immediately. But Marissa still blamed me.

Anyway, it felt good to strike back once in a while.

Not that it really got me anywhere in the long run.

I should have been used to that kind of confrontation after so long. But it just never got any easier. Suddenly feeling very weary, I closed my locker. It was time to get to class.

I found A.J. after homeroom to hand over Eggbert. "He had a good night," I joked. "Slept through without crying once. Your turn to baby-sit."

"Oh, great." A.J. grinned. "That means he'll be hyper all day and won't want to take a nap."

I giggled. "Those are the breaks. Are we still on for dinner with my mom tonight?"

He nodded. "Definitely." He kind of saluted me as he walked away, and I had to keep myself from grinning. But my smile faded as A.J. caught up with Fuzzy and they disappeared around a corner together.

For a second I'd almost forgotten that other people existed—people like Fuzzy and Jake and Marissa. A.J.'s friends, who also happened to be my enemies.

Things would be so much easier if it were just the two of us. . . .

I sighed and turned the other way, heading toward my first class. Maybe I was deluding myself to imagine that there could ever be anything real between me and A.J. That our friendship could ever go beyond just being partners in a stupid school project. Whenever I started to think it might be possible, something came along to remind me that we lived in different worlds.

And he had no idea how lonely my world could be sometimes.

A.J.'s visit to my house that night began sort of awkwardly. When he arrived, I tried to help him unwind his scarf, which was really long and tightly wrapped. I don't know why I did it, really—he was a big boy, and perfectly capable of doing it himself. But before I knew what I was doing, I found myself reaching for him, stepping closer. . . .

Suddenly realizing what he might be thinking, I gulped nervously. When I glanced up at his face, he was gazing at me with this sort of yearning look. His eyes mesmerized me—they were so intense, so open.

Then his face started moving closer, and I knew he was going to kiss me. Part of me wanted to stand there and let him. But another part—the part that had been hurt, over and over, since coming to Fairview—knew that was a seriously bad idea. I'd learned not to kiss any guy I wasn't sure I could trust. And I wasn't sure I could trust A.J. Not yet.

I jumped back in a panic. The only problem was, I was still holding on to his scarf. He let out a gargling noise, like he was being choked. Mostly because he was. He windmilled his arms and scrabbled to free himself from the scarf. I jumped forward to help and ended up tripping him instead.

He tried to keep his balance, but it was no use. He toppled forward, too fast for me to get out of the way. We ended up piled in the antique armchair we inherited from my great-grandmother.

I gasped for breath as the weight of his body pressed against my chest. My heart was pounding, and I felt paralyzed. All I could do for the first split second was stare into his eyes, which were mere inches from mine.

Then he hauled himself off me and we both stood up, brushing ourselves off and mumbling flustered apologies. My face was burning, and there were bright spots of color on both his cheeks too.

"Andie! Are you bringing your friend inside, or are you keeping him out in the cold all night long?"

I'd never been so glad to hear my mother's voice. Calling back that we were on our way, I led A.J. back to the kitchen.

The rest of the evening went a lot better. Mom and A.J. hit it off right away, chatting about school and Chicago and other stuff like old pals. I was glad. Mom's the most important person in my life, and A.J. . . . well, I wasn't sure how important he was going to turn out to be. But I was glad they were getting along.

"So, A.J.," Mom said at one point, somewhere around second helpings, "Andie tells me your mother teaches math over at the university."

"Yes, she loves it."

"And how about you?" Mom asked. "Are you going to follow in her footsteps and become a professor?"

A.J. looked a little uncomfortable. "Uh, I'm really not sure yet," he said. "I don't know what I want to do."

I jumped to his rescue. "Hey, what's the rush, Mom?" I asked lightly. "You're the one who's always saying I shouldn't rush into anything."

"Yes, that's true." Mom nodded. "You kids have lots of time. I wish I'd taken a little more time to enjoy myself when I was young."

"Oh, no. Now Mom's going to launch into her be-careful-not-to-make-the-same-mistakes-I've-made speech," I said with a mock groan.

Mom raised an eyebrow at me, then picked up the salad bowl and began to clear the table. "I do know better than you, smarty pants. It's what happens when you become a mother."

I reached over to pat Eggbert, who was beside my plate, nestled in the box A.J. had set up for him. "I know, I know," I said with a grin.

Mom rolled her eyes as A.J. and I laughed. "Fine," she said with a sniff and a pretend frown. "In that case, I'll leave you two wise parents to your project."

A.J. and I offered to help clean up, but she waved us away. So we headed into the den to get to work.

I tensed up when we were alone again, trying not to think about how close together we were sitting. As I pulled out my psych notebook and looked over our budget, I mentally chided myself for getting so freaked out just because I was alone in the den with a guy. I guess the last few months had made me a little paranoid.

Luckily, A.J. didn't seem to notice how jumpy I was. We talked about the budget and made some adjustments, but the whole time I kept thinking

about the Valentine's Day dance and what Marissa had said about Lauren Epps liking A.J. If he didn't ask her to the dance soon, would she ask him? Lauren wasn't exactly shy. She knew how to go out and get what she wanted.

If she asks him, will he say yes? I sneaked a quick glance at A.J. He was poring over a column of numbers on the budget, frowning slightly in concentration.

Will he go with her? Will they slow-dance together to every song? Will he kiss her good night afterward? Run his hands through her long, dark hair?

That line of thought was making me feel hot and sort of itchy all over, so I did my best to stop it. But it wasn't easy.

After a while Mom brought us dessert, and I started to relax once again. Pie and ice cream will do that every time. A.J. and I started chatting again. It started off light, but after a few minutes I found myself sort of pouring out my heart to him. I guess it was something about those deep, understanding brown eyes of his. Anyway, I told him how hard it seemed just to get through the day sometimes.

"Everything can be going along okay," I said slowly, almost forgetting that he was in the room as I thought back over the past few months. "And then you make one mistake—or one decision that doesn't even seem like a mistake at the time—and everyone turns on you."

He bit his lip and nodded uncertainly. For a second I thought he was going to say something comforting.

But he responded in a very different way. Taking

18

my face in his hand, he pulled me toward him. Before I knew what was happening, our lips had found each other and I had forgotten who I was.

Kissing him felt as easy as sinking into the most comfortable chair in the world. And as exhilarating as racing through the waves in a speedboat. Actually, it was both those feelings at once, and several more besides. As he buried one hand in my hair and slid the other around my waist, I felt as though I could stay right there, kissing him, forever.

Suddenly an image of A.J. falling into step with Fuzzy in the hall that day floated into my mind, and I snapped out of it. Fast. Shoving him away, I gasped for breath. "Why did you do that?" I demanded, feeling as though I might burst into tears.

He stammered through some kind of response, but I was hardly listening. *Was this because of the stuff I said about feeling alone?* I wondered. *Did he think that was some kind of come-on?*

If so, maybe it was my fault. I didn't know why I'd expected him to understand what it felt like to be me. How could he possibly know what it was like to be so lonely, to feel like you didn't fit in? He'd moved here and within a day or two he was hanging with the coolest kids in school.

I couldn't deal with it anymore. I needed time to think. To figure out what had just happened and what to do about it. "It's getting late." With great effort, I managed to keep my voice steady. "I should probably get started on my other homework."

He got up obediently and followed me toward

the foyer. After a quick discussion of the next phase of our project, he left.

After I'd closed the door behind him, I slumped against it, sliding down until I was sitting on the floor with my chin on my knees.

"What's wrong with me?" I muttered, pressing both hands to my forehead and willing my head to stop spinning. I had to get a grip. I couldn't practically pass out every time a guy kissed me. I'd handled those situations before—all too many times, in fact. I was practically an old pro.

But this wasn't just any guy. It was A.J. And admit it or not, I was really falling for him.

That was the part I wasn't sure I could handle.

Three

WEDNESDAY AFTERNOON I hurried home
after my shift at the library to get ready for
the housework part of our project. I'd invited A.J.
over then because I knew Mom was working late
and we'd have the place to ourselves. Mom was
kind of a fanatic when it came to cleaning—she
would probably try to pitch in to help us and end
up doing it all herself.

I was doubly glad Mom wasn't there when A.J.
arrived and confessed that he barely knew one end of
a mop from the other. I laughed as I imagined how
scandalized my mother would be at that. She had always insisted that I help with everything. I knew that
was partly out of necessity—since it was just the two
of us and she worked long hours, teamwork was the
only way things would get done. It wasn't like we
could afford to hire a cleaning service.

But I also knew that even if Mom had won the

lottery, she would still have expected me to help with the cooking and cleaning and home repairs. She believed that knowing how to do those things was part of being a self-sufficient, independent person.

I showed A.J. how to work the mop. After standing back and watching his technique for a moment, I nodded with satisfaction. "You catch on quick," I said. "I guess I can trust you alone with our kitchen floor. I'll go start on the vacuuming."

"Okay," he agreed, glancing up briefly before returning his attention to his work.

I left the room and headed for the utility closet to get the vacuum cleaner, feeling this sort of warm glow inside of me. This felt nice. Me and A.J., working as a team.

I spent the next fifteen minutes lost in a haze of daydreams, mostly about my possible future with A.J. Including the near future of the rest of that evening. Cleaning the house together wasn't exactly what most people would think of as a romantic evening, but I couldn't help wondering if he would kiss me again.

I was still a little confused about what had happened the night before. *Did he kiss me because he likes me?* I wondered.

Or did he do it because he thought he was going to get somewhere? Because Fuzzy and his other jerky friends told him I was a sure thing?

But that didn't make sense. *Even a muscle-headed moron like Fuzzy wouldn't be stupid enough to think he was going to score with my mother in the next room,* I thought. *Let alone*

someone sweet and smart like A.J. . . .

I sighed, trying to stay rational as I wound the cord around the handle of the vacuum and pushed it toward the den. It was tempting to go with my gut and believe that A.J. was just as nice as he seemed. But I had to be careful. I'd learned the hard way what could happen if I wasn't careful.

Still, as I headed for the kitchen to see what A.J. was doing, my thoughts wandered forward a little farther into the future—namely, to the Valentine's Day dance. Would Lauren Epps get her way and end up as A.J.'s date? Or might he possibly . . .

My thoughts trailed off as I entered the kitchen and saw that A.J. was still bent over the mop, attacking the floor as if it were covered in grime and muck instead of sparkling so brightly that it was almost blinding.

"A.J., you're going to wear out the floor!" I exclaimed, laughing.

He turned and blinked at me. "Huh?"

I grinned, amused and charmed by the perplexed expression on his adorable face. "You've been mopping for fifteen minutes. Every germ in town is on the run by now."

He grinned back. "I just wanted to make sure I did a good job." He leaned the mop against the counter and stretched.

"You did a great job," I told him, a little distracted by the sight of his muscles rippling under his thin T-shirt. "But come on. There's a whole lot of house left to clean."

23

"Huh?" he said again. He seemed a little distracted himself all of a sudden. I guessed he'd been so caught up in what he was doing that it was taking him a few seconds to snap out of it. That happened to me sometimes when I was shelving at the library. I was about to say something like that when I saw A.J. take a step forward—right toward the mop handle.

"Look out!" I yelled.

But it was too late. He tripped over the handle, and when he tried to save himself by lurching forward with his other foot, he crashed into the water bucket and sent it flying. Then he went flying himself, landing right in the puddle of water with a splash and a grunt.

It was so much like something out of a bad sitcom that I burst out laughing. He was soaked from head to toe, the mop leaning crazily over one shoulder, the bucket overturned near his feet. I laughed so hard I thought I would give myself a hernia.

"Very nice," he said with a groan as he pushed himself upright and ran his hands over his sopping hair. "Very sympathetic, Foster."

I apologized immediately, feeling a little guilty. But he wasn't hurt or anything, and he didn't really seem annoyed with me for being so amused by his misfortune. In fact, he was a really good sport about it.

I helped him to his feet, catching my breath as our hands touched. To cover that, I quickly offered to grab him some dry clothes from upstairs and hurried out of the room.

I went upstairs, suddenly realizing that I had no

idea what to bring him to wear. Mom and I were much smaller than A.J., so any of our pants or sweats were out. I supposed I could loan him my white terry-cloth bathrobe. It might be big enough. But I couldn't help blushing at the idea of A.J. wrapping my favorite comfy old robe around his naked body.

That was when I remembered that we had one other bathrobe in the house that would definitely fit him. It was an oversized robe that my crazy aunt Sue sent Mom for Christmas a couple of years ago. I think the last time they saw each other must have been when Mom was pregnant with me, because the robe was about four sizes too big. It was also hideous— pink chenille with daisies appliquéd onto the pockets.

Hurrying into Mom's bedroom, I started digging into the stacks of clothes on the closet shelf, praying that the robe was still there. It was. Sometimes it pays to have a mother who doesn't believe in throwing anything away.

Tucking the hideous pink bundle under one arm, I raced back downstairs. A.J. was waiting in the kitchen, still trying to squeeze water out of his hair and clothes. I handed over the robe.

I grinned at the look of dismay on his face when he saw it. "It's pink," he said helplessly.

"It's practically a family heirloom," I lied, "so be careful what you say about it."

"But it's pink!" He seemed unable to get past that fact.

I shrugged. "Sorry, it's the biggest robe I have. And you have really, um, broad shoulders."

He didn't say anything more after that, though he was blushing furiously as I pointed him toward the laundry room down the hall. While I waited for him to change, I quickly cleaned up the mess in the kitchen and put away the mop. Meanwhile, I tried not to think about the fact that A.J. was just a few yards away, peeling off his wet clothes. . . .

Ugh! I thought, squeezing my eyes shut and willing the images out of my head. I finished straightening up and then headed to the refrigerator to find us some sodas or something. *Maybe all those gossips out there aren't totally wrong about me. I do seem to be developing a dirty mind—at least ever since I met A.J.*

Suddenly I heard a muffled thump from somewhere toward the back of the house. I jumped, almost dropping the pitcher of lemonade I'd just pulled out of the fridge. "What was that?" I muttered.

My first thought was of A.J. in the laundry room. Had he somehow managed to trip again? Maybe fallen into the dryer or something?

But a second, smaller thump followed the first, and this time I was sure it was coming from outside the house. I was about to go and investigate when A.J. hurried back into the kitchen wrapped in the pink robe.

I had to smile again when I saw him. That robe would make almost anyone look like a frumpy housewife. At the same time, though, my gaze was drawn to the tiny triangle of his chest that was peeking out from the collar of the robe.

For a second I wanted to reach out and touch his skin, just to see what it felt like.

I shuddered, mentally smacking myself for the thought. I could just imagine what Fuzzy and the other guys would say if they could read my mind right then.

Another sound came from the backyard. This time it was more like a crash. "Did you hear that? It sounds like someone's in the backyard."

A.J. gazed at me and shrugged. "I don't think so," he said. "It was probably just the dryer."

I was sure it wasn't the dryer. But I shrugged. Why sweat it? It was probably just some kids cutting across our yard.

So then why was I getting the sudden chilly, squirmy, uncomfortable feeling that A.J. was lying to me about that sound for some unknown reason?

I had no idea. But the feeling was like a whole bucketful of cold, greasy water trickling down my back.

The next day, as usual, I headed to the school's small media library to eat my lunch. I'd been avoiding the cafeteria like the plague for months now, and not only because the smell of reheated meat loaf and veggie mush made me slightly ill. Ever since the rumors had started flying about me, walking into that huge room full of my schoolmates made me feel just like Mary, Queen of Scots, must have felt when she was being led to her execution at Fotheringhay Castle.

That didn't mean I hadn't been thinking lately

about giving it another try. Would A.J. invite me to sit with him if I showed up? Or would he leave me to wander alone to a table in the corner while he continued laughing and joking around with his friends? I thought I knew the answer to that. But I wasn't certain enough to take the chance. Not yet.

I sat down at the battered desk near the small room's only window and unwrapped the sandwich I'd made myself that morning. I was just chewing my first bite when I heard the door open. I glanced up, expecting to see Wendell Owen or Jeremy Price or one of the other AV guys coming in. They were just about the only people in school who ever talked to me like I was a regular person. They were also the only ones who usually showed up in the media library during lunch.

Instead I saw Lauren Epps walking into the room. She looked as surprised to see me as I was to see her. "Hi, Andie. What are you doing here?"

I immediately felt defensive, though her words and voice had been totally neutral. "What does it look like I'm doing?" I snapped. "I'm eating my lunch."

"Oh." She was glancing around at the floor-to-ceiling shelves that lined three sides of the room, looking confused. If she noticed my obnoxious response, she didn't show it. "Wow. This place is packed. Maybe I should wait and ask Mr. Jordan to help me."

Mr. Jordan, one of the English teachers, was in charge of the media library. He was also the director of the upcoming school musical, *Camelot*. Like everyone else in school, I knew that Lauren had been cast in the lead female role.

"Uh, what do you need?" I asked, feeling guilty about snapping at her. "Maybe I could help you out."

"Really?" She smiled at me tentatively. "That would be so great. I'm trying to find out what kind of costume Guinevere might've really worn. Because the costume people aren't really that into it—I'm afraid if I don't get involved, I'll just end up in somebody's old prom gown."

I stared at Lauren in surprise. She was the last person I would have suspected might be interested in extra research, even for one of her plays. "So you're here looking for videos about Arthurian costumes?" I asked, just to make sure I was getting it right.

She shrugged. "Videos, CD-ROMs, whatever. You don't think they have a copy of the movie version of the play, do you?" Her face brightened.

I chuckled. "Nope, sorry," I said. "Anyway, if you're serious about this . . ." I hesitated, not sure I should bother to continue. Why do Lauren Epps any favors? She and her whole crowd had given me the cold shoulder since day one.

"What?" she asked eagerly, brushing back a strand of long auburn hair that had come loose from her French braid. "Please, Andie. I'd do anything to get this figured out."

I winced, waiting for the punch line. *I'd do anything. Just like you, Andie. Just like you'll do anything with any guy who comes along.*

But she didn't say anything like that. She just gazed at me beseechingly. "Andie?" she said. "What were you going to say? Can you help me out? Please?"

"Sure," I said, letting out the breath I'd been holding. Why not? What more could Lauren and the others do to me, anyway? "They have some really amazing costume books at the university library. I could show them to you sometime if you want."

Lauren gasped. "That would be so nice!" she exclaimed enthusiastically. "You know, Andy's right about you. You are totally smart!"

I gulped at her mention of A.J.'s name. "Uh, Andy talks about me?"

"Sure." Lauren shrugged. "You're his partner for that psych marriage thingie, right?" She sighed. "You're so lucky. I wish I were in the same psych class as him. I would've, like, bribed the teacher or something so she'd make me his partner."

I had no idea what to say to that. But I could feel my cheeks turning pink as I remembered my little chat with Marissa the day before. Obviously she'd been right about Lauren's crush on A.J.

"So anyway," Lauren said brightly, not noticing my consternation, "we should figure out a time to get together at the library. I don't have my date book with me, but maybe we can talk later. Are you going to the basketball game tonight?"

I hesitated. A.J. and I were planning to take care of the dating part of our project that evening. Maybe going to the game together would be fun.

"The basketball game?" Marissa's haughty voice interrupted my thoughts. Glancing up quickly, I saw that she was standing in the doorway with her

hands on her hips, staring at me malevolently. "Why bother? Unless you're hoping to bag the team mascot too, sweetie?" She smirked at me.

Lauren gasped and turned on her friend. "Just because you blew it with Jake doesn't mean you have to take out your bad mood on Andie."

Marissa rolled her eyes. "Please, Lauren," she drawled. "Cut the polite act. Or don't you even care that she's getting busy with all the eligible guys in this school?" With that, she turned on her heel and walked back out of the room.

I scowled after her, furious.

"Sorry about that, Andie." Lauren shot me a sympathetic look. "Marissa's just still mad about— well, you know. She's not really a bad person."

"Whatever." I had my own opinion about that. But unlike certain other people, I could keep my opinions to myself.

"Anyway, like I said, we'll have to figure out a time to meet," Lauren said. She smiled. "And don't worry, I definitely don't mind if Andy is there too. You know, if you two are working on your project or whatever, I could just sort of tag along." She winked at me, and I smiled weakly.

So that's her angle, I thought. *She thinks I can help her get to know A.J. better. I wonder if she really wandered in here totally clueless. Maybe she found out I eat here every day, and planned out this whole little "accidental" encounter. . . .*

I didn't bother to finish the thought. Suddenly I was too tired. Tired of always worrying about people's

real motives. Being suspicious of everyone. Being on my guard all the time.

Maybe Lauren had some ulterior motives. But she'd been nicer to me than any of the girls at school had been in a long time. She'd even told off Marissa on my behalf. No matter what the reason, I appreciated that.

These days, I could use all the friendly faces I could get.

Four

T HAT AFTERNOON AT the library, I was at the reception desk sorting the mail when I heard light, rapid footsteps approaching. When I glanced up, Courtney Calhoun was standing there smiling down at me, to my intense surprise. Her bouncy blond hair was pulled back, with just a few strands tumbling down to frame her face. It looked great that way. I almost wished I could ask her to show me how to do it to my hair. But that was a foolish thought. It was the kind of thing you would ask a friend.

"Hi, Andie," she said in her high, chirping voice. "How's it going?"

"Hi," I returned her greeting cautiously. "Uh, I'm fine. How are you?"

"Great. Can I talk to you for a second?"

"Sure." I scanned the reception area, wondering if Kyle and Jake and Fuzzy and Marissa were

hiding somewhere, laughing at me from behind a book cart. But the place was almost empty, and I didn't see anyone from school.

Courtney leaned forward across the desk, peering at me curiously. "Is there something wrong with your neck?"

"My neck?"

"Yeah, you're stretchirg it from side to side like they do in my yoga class. It makes me dizzy." Courtney shrugged and cracked her gum. "Anyway, I was talking to Lauren earlier, and she told me how you work here, and how you're, like, really smart and everything."

"Yes?" I said cautiously, not quite sure what she was driving at. Was she afraid I was going to lure her boyfriend, Kyle, into my den of sin with my devastating intelligence, or entice him with my knowledge of the Dewey decimal system? Somehow I didn't think so. Kyle Bladen was just about the only guy in that crowd who had never hit on me. That was no surprise. It was easy to see that he was totally smitten with Courtney.

Courtney tugged on one hoop earring thoughtfully. "Well, I was thinking about this egg project. I could really use a decent grade on it, and I figured it wouldn't hurt to jazz up our written report somehow. Kyle already asked his cousin to help us design a really cool cover. But I was thinking that it would be fun if we could also include sort of an introduction where we gave some interesting information on, like, the meaning of marriage

34

throughout the ages or whatever." She shrugged sheepishly. "So I went to the bookstore at the mall and looked around. But I guess I'm not that great at doing research, because I really didn't find anything good."

"That's a terrific idea," I told her, meaning it. "But I'm not surprised you didn't find much at the mall—that bookstore's a joke. I'm sure there are plenty of books about marriage here at the library, though. I could look some up for you if you want, and bring them into school tomorrow or Monday."

"That's so nice of you!" Courtney exclaimed, her voice squeaking so excitedly that one of the librarians, who was working at the computer nearby, glanced over at us and frowned disapprovingly. Courtney didn't notice. "I would, like, so totally appreciate that, Andie. Really. I'll even give you a credit in the footnotes of the report if you want."

"That's okay." I smiled at her enthusiasm. It was no wonder she was so popular. She practically bubbled over with energy and good spirits. "It's no big deal. I'm happy to do it."

"Thanks," Courtney said again. "You know, Andy's lucky to have you as a partner for this project. He's so smart, and you're so smart. . . ." She puffed out her cheeks in a little poof of a sigh. "Kyle and I are both kind of hopeless when it comes to schoolwork and stuff. Sometimes I sort of wish that Kyle was a little more like

35

Andy—you know, cute and cool but also, like, *responsible*. Kyle never takes school seriously, and that makes it harder for me to take it seriously, you know?"

Suddenly I realized that Courtney was having a real conversation with me. Me, Andie Foster. The girl most people at school avoided like the plague when they weren't saying nasty things to me.

While I was pondering that, Courtney cocked her head to one side. "That reminds me. I hope you don't mind my asking," she said, "but are you naturally smart, or do you have to work at it?"

"Uh—what?" Still, thinking about my own reputation, I wasn't following her new line of conversation.

"You know, your good grades." Courtney shrugged and pushed her bright blond hair out of her face. "I mean, you seem to get A's just naturally, you know? Meanwhile, I work my patootie off and wind up with a B-minus or a C. How do you do it?"

What could I say to a question like that? *Maybe if you spent more time studying and less time hanging out at Moe's or making out in your boyfriend's Mustang, you'd get more A's yourself.*

No, I wasn't about to be that rude, especially when Courtney was actually being friendly to me for the first time ever. "Uh, I don't know," I said helplessly. "I guess it's sort of a combination of things."

It was a pretty lame response, but Courtney nodded. "Yeah, you've probably been working at it a long time," she said thoughtfully. "I only started taking school seriously this year, when I decided I wanted to be a nurse. But it's kind of hard to make up for ten years of goofing around in just two years. I only hope I get accepted into nursing school somewhere."

"I'm sure you will," I assured her, meaning every word. Courtney would probably make a fantastic nurse. She already had the people skills down cold. "Those schools won't hold the past against you, not if you're serious about nursing now."

"Thanks." Courtney actually seemed grateful for my vote of confidence. She smiled at me. "You're sweet to say that. Anyway, are you sure it's all right? Finding me those books, I mean."

"Definitely no problem," I said. "I know every inch of this library. I'll just search the computer filing system under *marriage* and then sift the results by a few other keywords to narrow it down before I . . ." She sighed loudly, and I trailed off, fearing I was boring her.

But when Courtney sighed again, I realized she was actually impressed by what I was saying. "That's amazing. I wish I were talented like you. But my parents say my gifts come from other areas, that I have a real way with people." She smiled. "I think that means I'm a C student who's popular."

I returned her smile ruefully. "Hey, there are worse things than that."

She gazed at me shrewdly. "Yeah," she said. "I guess there are. But listen, you really shouldn't let gossip get you down too much. I mean, people are always calling me an airhead behind my back." She shrugged. "Sometimes to my face, even. I don't let it bother me."

"That's not really the same thing," I said stiffly. Who was Courtney Calhoun to advise me on how to run my life? She didn't have my problems. She had lots of friends and a cute boyfriend who worshiped the ground she walked on.

She shrugged again. "Maybe not," she said. "Now that you mention it, it kind of stinks that people are always talking about you that way. After all, Jake and Fuzzy are after a new girl every week, and nobody gives them a hard time about it." She blinked her wide hazel eyes thoughtfully, pondering that one for a second. "Personally, I think you should be able to do what you want to do without being hassled for it. With Andy or whoever."

For a moment I was so surprised that she was sticking up for me—sort of—that I almost missed part of what she'd said. Then it sank in. "Wait a minute," I said. "I haven't done anything with Andy. We've just been working on our project."

That was almost the truth. I figured a couple of kisses didn't count.

Courtney held up her hands appeasingly. "Hey, you don't have to be coy with me," she said. "I

don't blame you for being into Andy. He's adorable." She giggled and fluttered her eyelashes. "If it were me, I'd probably be ripping his clothes off too."

I frowned. I was starting to get a really bad feeling about this. "Courtney," I said, "what are you trying to say here? Have people been—been talking about me and Andy?"

Courtney looked surprised. "All I know is what I heard from Kyle and the guys," she said. "And I'm definitely not judging you or anything like that. All I'm trying to say is that after what Kyle told me about your extra-credit work with Andy—" She blushed and giggled. "That's what Kyle and I call it when we make out, extra-credit work. Anyway, after all that, I'm surprised you've had a chance to get as much of the project done as you have."

"A.J. and I haven't done any 'extra-credit work.'" I was so furious I could barely spit out the words. Who was spreading rumors about me now? Whoever it was, they were dead meat. I wasn't going to let any low-minded mouth breathers mess up what I had—or hoped I had, anyway— with A.J.

"I don't know. All the guys were joking around about it at lunch." Courtney shrugged. "Like, they said A.J. was walking around your house in, like, a pink robe yesterday. So what are we supposed to think?"

I froze. How did people know about that?

"Well," I said carefully, "they might think the truth. That we were doing the housework part of the project, and Andy is a real spaz when it comes to mopping. He got water all over his clothes, so I loaned him a robe while he dried them in the dryer."

Courtney studied me for a long moment. "Okay," she said. "That makes sense. I believe you."

"Good." I was on a roll now. "And while you're at it, let me also tell you something else. I never slept with any of those guys who said I did. They're all lying just to make themselves look like studs or something. I—I've never done *that* at all. With anyone. Including Andy."

This time Courtney looked kind of surprised. And remained silent for even longer. But finally she nodded. "I believe you," she said again. "Actually, I sort of suspected it anyway. You never really seemed like the type to me." She smiled tentatively. "You know, I'm glad I stopped in here to see you. It's been very—educational." She glanced around at the books surrounding us and grinned. "I guess it's true what Daddy always tells me. I could learn a whole lot if I just spent a little more time at the library."

I sort of went limp. It felt so good to tell someone the truth! And unless I was totally deluding myself, Courtney really did seem to be taking me at my word. It was such a strange, wonderful, almost totally forgotten feeling that I was literally

weak in the knees. "Thanks," I told her, wishing I knew how to express what it meant to me. "I'm really glad you stopped by too."

"Good." Courtney put one delicate hand on my arm and squeezed gently. "I'll catch you later, Andie, okay?" She headed toward the door, then paused and glanced back at me. "And just so you know, I'm going to tell all my friends the truth about you, now that I know it. I'm glad you told me."

I realized that under her dumb-blonde image, Courtney was one of the nicest, most confident, and, yes, *smartest* girls I had ever met. "Thanks," I said. "Thanks a lot."

"No big." She looked at her watch. "I've got to go and meet Kyle before the game." She giggled. "He claims he can't shoot straight unless we get in some extra-credit work beforehand. If you know what I mean." She waggled her perfectly shaped eyebrows at me and winked. "Talk to you later."

I watched her walk toward the exit, her perky hips swaying suggestively as she walked, as usual. I contemplated what she'd told me the guys had been saying. Could it really be as bad as she'd made it sound? And where did they get their information, anyway? Could A.J.—nice, sweet, sensitive, smart A.J.—be telling all his buddies that he was rocking my world every night?

I couldn't quite believe it. But suddenly the thought of meeting him for our date in a couple of

41

hours made me even more nervous than I'd been before.

One thing's for sure, I thought grimly, remembering Marissa's harsh words. *A.J. and I are definitely not going to be showing up at that basketball game tonight!*

Despite my conversation with Courtney, I decided to dress for that evening's activities as if A.J. and I really were going out on a nice, romantic date together. Over the past few months I'd had plenty of people judge me without having all the facts. I didn't want to do the same to him. *Innocent until proven guilty,* I told myself, repeating it until I actually started to believe it.

It took me a long time to decide on the right outfit to wear on our date. My usual look was pretty sporty and casual, especially in the winter. But tonight I wanted to dress up a little. Make sure A.J. couldn't help but notice me.

I finally settled on a sage-colored jersey dress that flattered my coloring, even though it was a little bare for February in Ohio. I didn't wear much makeup most of the time—just a little mascara and a touch of lip gloss—but tonight I carefully applied blush and some subtle eye shadow along with an extra coat of gloss. I even spritzed on some of Mom's favorite perfume. As I looked myself over in the full-length mirror on the back of my door, I couldn't help admitting that I looked pretty spectacular. My hair was behaving just right

for once, falling softly from my favorite barrettes in soft waves rather than being stick straight, as usual.

But as I continued to twist and turn in front of the mirror, trying to get a good look from every angle, I started to feel nervous again. Besides showing off my legs and flattering my slender waist and hips, the green dress displayed a lot more cleavage than I usually showed. Was it too much?

Would it make A.J. think the guys were right about me? Did it make me look pretty and sexy— or slutty?

Just as I was seriously considering changing into a turtleneck sweater and khakis, Mom poked her head into my room. "I'm on my way out," she started. "Have a nice— Oh, honey!" she gasped. "You look stunning!"

I looked down bashfully. "Really?" I cleared my throat. "I was afraid it might be, um, too much."

"Oh, sweetie, no! It's perfect!" She hurried in and tugged gently at the shoulder of the dress, smoothing out a small wrinkle. "You look absolutely lovely. A.J. is going to go gaga over you!"

I hoped she was right. But Mom didn't know about my problems at school. Still, it was getting late. I had to leave if I didn't want to keep A.J. waiting.

Taking a deep breath, I smiled at my mother. "Thanks, Mom," I said. "I'll walk you out, okay?"

Less than ten minutes later, I was standing just inside the door at Moe's, my coat and sweater over my arm. It was warm in the diner—almost stuffy, especially after the brisk evening air outside. But I suspected that the temperature wasn't the only reason I was practically sweating.

I didn't have long to wait. As usual, A.J. was right on time. He burst through the door and glanced around at the booths and tables, obviously looking for me.

I cleared my throat to catch his attention. He turned and spotted me right away.

His jaw dropped—literally—when he got a look at me. "Wow," he said, his gaze slipping from my face down the length of my body before shooting back up again to meet my eyes. "Uh, you look great."

"Thanks." I felt a little uncomfortable. On one hand, I was pleased that he so obviously found me attractive. But at the same time, I was still worried about what message my outfit might be sending to him. "Hey, I'm starved. Let's find a table."

Things remained a little awkward between us at first. But then I guess we both sort of forgot that this was a date, and we started talking just as easily as we always did. Once in a while A.J.'s eyes still dipped down to take in the scenery below my neck, but after a while I stopped worrying about that. It wasn't like he was leering at me the way Fuzzy had that afternoon back in September. He certainly wasn't pawing at me or suggesting we go somewhere private.

In fact, as the evening wore on, I found myself feeling surprisingly comfortable. I was actually enjoying our date—hanging out in a public place with A.J. was nice. A bunch of other kids from school were there—mostly the smarter and artsier crowd, since the popular kids were all at the basketball game.

Occasionally one of them would glance over at us, and Jeremy Price even stopped by our table to ask me about some homework. But for once I wasn't totally self-conscious, wondering if they were all whispering about me behind their menus. It was almost like the past few months had never happened.

Almost.

A.J. and I were just polishing off a yummy chocolate sundae when the diner's door burst open and a whole gang of kids poured in, talking and laughing at the top of their lungs. I grimaced as I recognized them. The cool kids.

My heart sank, and the old anxious feelings were back in a flash. *Why did I agree to come to this place?* I wondered desperately, my whole body going tense. *It's not the only restaurant in town. And everyone knows the basketball players and their groupies always come here after the games.*

Before I could figure out how a supposedly smart girl like me could have been so stupid, Jake had spotted us. He came loping over to our table, a grin on his broad, cold-reddened face. He greeted A.J. and shot me a curious glance. But

45

before he could say much else, Veronica Morita caught up to him and grabbed his arm possessively.

"Hey," she snapped, casting me a suspicious glance. "Where do you think you're going?" She began haranguing him about their psych project. The two of them were "married," which was a big joke. It was obvious that Jake still had the hots for Marissa, even though she'd dumped him like an old, worn-out pair of shoes. And Veronica was so vain that I doubted she cared which guy took her out, as long as he complimented her clothes and hair.

After a moment Jake managed to shoo Veronica back to the rest of their group, which had settled around a table near the center of the room. Then he leaned against the edge of our booth and started doing what he did best—goofing around.

Then the door opened again, admitting Marissa along with a blast of arctic air. Very appropriate, if you ask me.

"Hey," Jake said, suddenly dropping his whole idiot-clown routine. "Listen, I've got to go. If wifey comes looking for me, tell her I'm in the john."

"Uh-oh," A.J. joked as Jake hurried toward Marissa and started fawning all over her. "Looks like someone's marriage is in some serious trouble."

I wasn't amused. Jake certainly knew how to

cause trouble—and not just for himself. Thanks to him and the rest of the jock posse, I was nothing more than a dirty joke to most of Fairview High. "We'd better get going," I said shortly, not wanting to think about all that. Not now, when I was trying to have a nice time with A.J. "The movie starts soon, and we don't want to miss the previews."

A.J. seemed a little confused—not surprising, since we still had plenty of time to make the movie—but he agreed and called for the check. Soon we were at the register. I waited impatiently while A.J. paid the bill—like a true gentleman, he'd insisted on picking up the tab. With some effort, I kept my gaze on A.J. and the cashier, refusing to glance over at the raucous group at the jocks' table.

Just when I thought we were going to make a clean escape, Fuzzy and Kyle came bounding over. "Yo, Parker," Fuzzy said, glancing at me with a leer. I'd put my sweater on over my dress, but I still felt naked as he ran his eyes over my entire body, finally settling on my legs. Unfortunately, I had no way to hide them. "Where'd Jake go?" he added, moistening his lips and taking a step closer to me.

I stepped back, glaring at him. He wiggled his eyebrows at me suggestively before his gaze locked onto my legs again.

"I'm not sure," A.J. said calmly.

I glanced over at Kyle. He might have been

devoted to Courtney, but that wasn't stopping him from letting his dark brown eyes take a leisurely tour down me from head to toe. Or at least from chest to leg. "Well," he said with a sly smile, "at least we know he didn't sneak off to the alley to boink your wife, since she's still here."

I gasped. I hadn't seen that one coming at all, and it felt as though someone had just plunged a dagger into my heart. I had to turn my face away so none of the guys would see the scalding tears that had rushed to my eyes. Blinking hard, I managed to get them under control. But I still felt hot all over, trapped by the flames of shame and humiliation that were rolling over and through me.

I was so upset that I almost didn't hear what A.J. said next. "Lay off, man," he snapped, sounding angrier than I'd ever heard him. Shooting him a quick look, I saw him take a step toward Kyle. "That was a totally harsh thing to say."

"What's with you?" Kyle asked, looking confused. "I was just goofing with you."

"Well, I don't think it's funny," A.J. snapped. "In fact, I think you owe Andie an apology."

Kyle looked annoyed. He took a threatening step toward A.J., and I almost screamed, sure that he was going to flatten him. But suddenly he seemed to change his mind.

"Oh," he said. "Right. Sorry about that, man." He patted A.J. on the shoulder before turning to me. "Sorry," he said with a sheepish smile. "Guess that was pretty, uh, rude."

I shrugged, not quite believing that he meant it. Still, I was glad that Kyle and Fuzzy at least respected A.J. enough to pretend they respected me too.

A.J. put his arm around me. He glanced at me, his face so caring and concerned that I almost felt like crying again. When was the last time that anyone, except maybe my mother, had looked at me that way? It was as if he really wanted to look right down deep inside of me, find where I was hurt, and fix it.

"Come on," he told me gently. "We should get going."

I nodded, glancing down at my feet. I didn't dare hold his gaze. If I did, I might just start to bawl, right there in front of the entire restaurant. And I couldn't let that happen. The only thing I still had left at school was my pride.

I needed to buy some time to pull myself together. "Give me a second, okay?" I told him thickly. "I just want to stop in the rest room."

I fled to the relative safety of the ladies' room. As long as Lauren or Veronica or one of the other girls didn't decide to come in and powder her nose in the next few minutes, I would be okay.

Gripping the cool, smooth edge of the sink, I stared at myself in the slightly grimy mirror. *Why me?* I wondered. *What did I ever do to deserve this life?*

I had no idea what the answer was, and when it came right down to it, I didn't care that much. I

just wanted it to stop. That feeling I'd had for a while, before Jake and the others came in—I wanted to have that feeling all the time. Why couldn't I seem to do anything to make it happen? It wasn't fair.

Life's not fair, sweetie. It was my mother's voice speaking in my head—sadly, slowly, sounding just the way it had when she'd told me my father wasn't coming back from his latest business trip. I hadn't really understood at the time—I was only five years old—but now, looking back, my heart broke for her. And for myself too.

Still, I reminded myself that my mom didn't need or want my pity. Not anymore. She'd rebuilt her life. I knew it hadn't been easy for her, but she hadn't let anything anyone else said or did stop her. All I could do was try to follow her example.

Neither A.J. nor I mentioned the little scene with Kyle and Fuzzy for the rest of the evening. Still, the nice vibe we'd had back at the diner was pretty much ruined. The movie we saw was a comedy, but I had to force myself to laugh at the funny parts. I didn't want A.J. to guess that I was still smarting over Kyle's obnoxious comment.

He wouldn't understand, anyway, I thought, sneaking a peek at A.J.'s profile in the darkened theater. *He would probably think I was being too sensitive. That Kyle was only kidding around and didn't mean any harm.*

I bit my lip to keep from snorting at the irony of that. Somehow the careless jokes and comments

that the majority of kids made were even harder to take than the outright meanness of the minority. At least Marissa had the guts to say exactly what she thought of me, and say it to my face.

Not that she would listen to anything I had to say in return, I thought bitterly, sinking down against the scratchy fabric of the theater seat. *She's already made up her mind about me, just like everyone else. And she's never going to forgive me for what Jake did at the homecoming dance.*

But just when I was ready to tumble into the familiar morass of helplessness, resentment, and depression, I suddenly remembered my little talk with Lauren at lunch that day. And Courtney's visit to the library after school. They had both talked to me like I was a real person—not an inflatable doll with no feelings to be hurt.

At least a couple of girls at Fairview seemed willing to give me a chance. And not just any girls. Lauren and Courtney were two of the most popular girls in school. If they decided they liked me, would it make other people like me too?

More important, would it make everyone believe that I wasn't the kind of person they thought I was, just because a few insecure guys had decided to use me to bolster their own pathetic egos?

Just then A.J. shifted in his seat beside me. A second later I caught a glimpse of his hand sliding over from his seat. I felt his fingers touch the thin fabric of my dress as he started exploring tentatively on my side of the armrest.

I stiffened for a second, assuming he was trying to cop a feel. But before I could slap his hand away, it found my hand, which had been resting on my knee. He took it and squeezed it lightly before pulling it over onto his own knee.

A warm feeling spread through me as his hand fell still again, still wrapped gently but firmly around mine. He wasn't putting the moves on me at all. He just wanted to hold my hand.

Call me a sap, but I couldn't help thinking that it was the most romantic thing anyone had ever done.

Five

I GLANCED AROUND the kitchen, which was already a total disaster area, even though the only thing I'd made so far was a tossed salad. I was very glad that Mom was working a double shift that day and wouldn't be home for hours. Tonight A.J. and I were finally having our home-cooked family dinner for our marriage project, and I wanted it to be special. Maybe even romantic.

Of course, that didn't mean that I didn't still harbor a small, slithery bit of doubt about A.J.'s feelings for me. Every time I thought about the way he had taken my hand during the movie, or how he'd stuck up for me at Moe's, or how tenderly he had kissed me as he dropped me off at home after the movie, I also remembered Fuzzy. He had seemed pretty great for a while too. Maybe not the sharpest knife in the drawer, but funny.

And sort of sweet in his own loudmouthed, goofy, obnoxious way.

I remembered all those nice things about him. But I also remembered how he'd scowled at me and called me a nasty name when I'd pushed his hands away from my blouse. And how he'd told everyone who would listen that I was easy—that I'd practically flung myself at him, in fact. And then I started remembering all the other guys who'd started out seeming to like me for me, but ended up ditching me as soon as they realized I wasn't going to give them what they really wanted.

But A.J.'s not like all those other guys, I tried to reassure myself as I greased a loaf pan. *Is he?*

The truth was, I just wasn't sure. I thought I knew the real A.J. But I couldn't seem to let my guard down enough to really test whether I could trust him. What was that saying? Once bitten, twice shy.

As I started to gather up the ingredients for the meat loaf I'd planned, I opened the refrigerator and realized that we were out of eggs, of all things. "Oh, man," I muttered, wishing that I'd decided to make spaghetti and meatballs instead. For a moment I considered ditching the whole cooking thing and suggesting we order a pizza. Ms. Church would never need to know.

But I couldn't do that. For one thing, I'd never cheated on a school assignment in my life. And even if A.J. was willing to cut corners—which I doubted, judging by his hard work on the rest of

the project so far—I certainly didn't want to give him any reason to doubt my character.

His buddies have already taken care of that, I thought. Then, pushing those familiar worries out of my mind, I turned off the stove and headed out of the kitchen to grab my coat and keys.

The Shop 'n' Save was crowded when I got there. I'd never realized that so many people did their grocery shopping on Saturday afternoon. Mom and I split the shopping duties along with all the other chores, but I usually ended up doing my share on the way home from work on weekday evenings. Ever since the rumors had brought my social life to a screeching halt, I'd preferred to keep Saturdays—my day off from the library—as quiet and private as possible, with little or no contact with the outside world.

Dodging a woman trying to keep a squirming toddler in the seat of her grocery cart, I headed straight for the refrigerated aisle on the end and quickly found a carton of grade-A jumbos. Then I made a beeline for the express lane. There were a few people ahead of me, but it wasn't until I'd picked up a magazine and started flipping through it that I realized that Courtney Calhoun was standing right in front of me.

She turned around a split second later, before I could slip away to another line. "Andie!" She actually sounded pleased to see me. "What are you doing here?"

I held up the box of eggs with a weak smile.

"Don't worry, I'm not trying to replace Andy junior," I joked lamely. "Just picking up a last-minute ingredient for our family dinner tonight. You know, for the project."

"Cool." To my intense relief, Courtney didn't make any suggestive comments about my "marriage" to A.J. or our romantic Saturday-night dinner. And if she was thinking anything along those lines, her wide-set hazel eyes didn't reveal it. "Hey, as long as you're here, can I ask you a question?"

"Sure."

Courtney pulled a shopping list out of her jacket pocket and wrinkled her nose. "Do you know if you're really supposed to put peppers in cream-of-mushroom soup?" She gestured at a large green bell pepper in the shopping basket at her feet. "Kyle and I are doing the cooking thing tonight too, and I swore I could make an appetizer all by myself, from scratch." She rolled her eyes. "He's an okay cook, but I've never tried to make anything more complicated than toast before. So of course he's totally acting like Mr. Superior. He almost refused to let me help at all, until I put my foot down." She frowned. "He can be so stubborn sometimes!"

I was a little surprised to hear Courtney talking about her beloved Kyle that way. "Oh, well," I said lightly, not sure what Courtney expected me to say. "I guess it's like Ms. Church was saying in class yesterday. Being married means being able to compromise."

"I guess so," Courtney said morosely. She sighed. "You know, I was thrilled when Kyle and I got matched together. But now I really can't wait for this stupid marriage project to end so we can forget all this responsibility and compromise stuff and just go back to being in love."

I hid a smile. Courtney wasn't making much sense, but I could sympathize with her feelings. Playing responsible grown-ups wasn't quite as easy as I'd thought it would be either. Part of what we were supposed to be doing was learning to communicate effectively with our partners. And I wasn't sure that A.J. and I were doing that. Otherwise, why would suspicions about his true motives keep popping into my head at all hours of the day?

I didn't say anything about that, though. Instead I just shook my head. "I don't think you want that kind of pepper," I told Courtney tactfully. "The recipe probably meant black pepper. You know, as in the stuff on the table next to the salt."

"Oh!" Courtney's expression cleared. "Of course." She laughed, sounding a bit sheepish. "It just said pepper, so of course I thought . . . well, anyway, I'm glad I ran into you." She grinned. "I never would have heard the end of it from Kyle if I'd gone ahead with this."

She leaned down and grabbed the green pepper, dropping it onto the little counter behind the register. Tucking her shopping list back in

her pocket, she shot me a grateful look.

"But this will just be our secret, right?" she asked.

"Sure." I smiled. "I'll never tell a soul."

"Thanks, Andie. You're a pal." Just then Courtney looked down and noticed the magazine I was holding. I glanced down too. To my dismay, it was open to a page with a large headline trumpeting "Snag the Guy of Your Dreams—in Five Easy Steps!"

Courtney giggled as I blushed and slapped the magazine shut. "Don't be embarrassed," she said. "I used to read articles like that all the time before I met my Kylie."

I was actually happy to hear her mentioning him so fondly again. "You're lucky," I told her. "Anyone can see he's really crazy about you."

"Thanks." She smiled contentedly. "You know, even though I was complaining about him just now, he really is the best most of the time. So romantic and everything. I can't wait for the Valentine's dance. . . . Oh!" She suddenly looked worried. "Um, you are going, aren't you?"

"I don't know." I willed myself not to blush. I certainly didn't want her to guess how much time I'd spent lately daydreaming about that stupid dance. I kept trying to picture what it would be like if A.J. asked me. Maybe he would send me a box of red roses with a romantic card inside asking me to be his Valentine at the Valentine's dance. Then again, it would be even sweeter if he asked

me in person, maybe surprising me by turning up on my doorstep some evening and begging me to be his date. . . .

"Oh, you have to go!" Courtney's high-pitched giggle snapped me back to reality. "It's going to be a blast. The school even hired a band this time instead of the lame DJ they usually get!"

"We'll see," I said noncommittally. She opened her mouth again, and I guessed she wasn't going to back down until I swore on my grandmother's grave that I would be there. I had to distract her somehow. My gaze fell on the cover of the magazine I was still holding, which featured a model in an elegant peach-colored gown. "Uh, what are you wearing to the dance?"

Courtney's face brightened, and I knew I'd struck gold. She chattered happily about her shopping plans for the next few minutes, until it was her turn at the register.

Then she briefly turned her attention to the pimply college-age guy ringing her up. She flirted with him effortlessly, making him blush and smile at the same time. I couldn't help admiring her technique.

I wish I could do that, I thought wistfully. *I wish I could flirt with a guy if I felt like it without making everyone think I was inviting him to hop into my bed.*

Then I sighed. What good had wishing ever done me?

Courtney turned to say good-bye as the cashier handed her the bag containing her purchases, brushing her hand with his own and then turning lobster red. I stepped forward to hand over my eggs.

"By the way," Courtney said, pausing as she started toward the door, "did you have a chance to look up those books you were talking about?"

I realized I hadn't. After she'd left the library the afternoon before, my boss had given me some rush orders to type into the computer. When that was finished, I'd started daydreaming about dancing the night away at the Valentine's dance with A.J., and my entire conversation with Courtney had flown straight out of my head.

"Not yet," I confessed. "I'm really sorry. I work the whole day tomorrow. I'll do it then, I promise."

"Okay, thanks."

"No, really," I insisted, still feeling guilty about forgetting. "I can drop them off at your house after my shift if you want."

"That's okay. You can just bring them to school on Monday if you want." She shrugged. "I trust you."

She waved brightly and turned to hurry off, but I stood stock-still, a little in shock from what she'd just said. *I trust you.* Wasn't trust what it was all about? There was the way I'd trusted Fuzzy, thinking he was my friend. And the other guys after them. I'd trusted them to have good,

kind intentions toward me. But they'd broken my trust in a big way, and now nobody in school trusted me to do anything right. Except for a few people. Courtney. Lauren. And maybe A.J.

They trusted me, or at least they seemed to. But could I trust them? Could I open myself up to that risk again?

"Miss?" I blinked, coming back to earth as I realized that the pimply-faced cashier was looking at me strangely. "Miss? Here's your change."

"Oh! Thanks," I mumbled. Grabbing my bag from him, I turned and hurried out of the store, doing my best to shake off my sudden philosophical mood. It was getting late, and I had a lot of cooking to do.

Normally I'm a decent cook. But that day I was so nervous that I was a total spaz. First I dropped the carton of eggs I'd just bought, cracking five out of the dozen. Then I knocked over the flour, making it look as though it had snowed in the sink.

Finally I managed to get it together long enough to slap together the meat loaf and shove it into the oven to bake. Wiping my hands on Mom's apron, which I'd borrowed to protect the nice sweater and pants I'd picked out for that evening, I looked around the disaster area that used to be my mom's nice, neat kitchen. Now plates and pots were piled in the sink, grease was spattered all over the stove, and flour and eggshells were everywhere.

Eggshells.

"Oh, no," I exclaimed aloud. "Eggbert!"

I glanced around frantically, searching for the plain white egg in its little box. Over the past week, it had become almost second nature to be aware of where it was at all times.

I couldn't have, I thought in horror, glancing at the empty shells on the counter. *I mean, I was pretty crazed. But still . . .*

Just as I was tempted to call Ms. Church and confess to being the worst egg mother in history, I remembered. A.J. had Eggbert today. He'd volunteered to take an extra turn egg-sitting, since I was doing all the cooking.

That's what compromise is all about, right? he'd joked as he'd tucked Eggbert's little box into his backpack.

I slumped against the counter, weak with relief. At that moment the doorbell rang, making me jump.

I glanced at my watch. "Yikes!" I muttered. "Dinnertime already." Whipping off Mom's apron, I hurried to open the door.

A.J. was standing on the front step, holding a bouquet of irises. He looked so cute and familiar and amiable that I relaxed instantly. "Hi," I said.

"Hi." Suddenly he was looking at me intently, in a way he'd never done before.

I wasn't sure what to say. All I could do was gaze back at him for a long moment. Neither of us spoke; we just stared at each other.

Finally A.J. sort of coughed. "Here," he said softly. "Uh, I brought flowers. For you."

"Thanks." I accepted the flowers and waved him inside. While I was facing away from him, shutting the door against the cold winter air, I took a few deep breaths, trying to calm down. Then I turned back toward him with a smile. "They're beautiful. Come on in. Dinner's almost ready. How's the baby?" I knew that he called our egg Junior, but I'd never actually told him that I thought of the little white fellow as Eggbert.

We headed into the kitchen. A.J. said something about Fuzzy almost sitting on Junior that day, and I rolled my eyes. "Sounds typical," I said, unable to keep my feelings about his friends to myself any longer. "Fuzzy always acts before he thinks." I sighed, hoping A.J. wouldn't get mad. But I just couldn't let this pass. "Let me tell you, I'm really glad I got you as a partner for this project instead of someone like Kyle or Fuzzy. I'm sorry, I know they're your friends, but sometimes they can be really immature."

He smiled uncomfortably and defended them, as usual, saying that they were just kidding around. *That may be true,* I thought as I turned to check on the potatoes I was boiling. Sticking a fork in one of them, I discovered that they were done. *But their kidding around has caused some all-too-serious problems for me.*

Still, I let it drop. I didn't want to ruin our evening.

I took the potatoes off the stove and checked on everything else. While the meat loaf finished cooking, we sat down to write our journal entry for that day. By the time we finished, the food was ready, so we sat down to eat. I even poured some ginger ale into a pair of wineglasses.

A.J. grinned. "What's this for?" he asked, picking up his glass and swirling the contents around as if it were really a glass of vintage chardonnay or something.

I raised my glass and smiled at him. "A toast to our project."

"I'll drink to that," he replied, clinking his glass softly against mine. "I'm really glad we're working together, Andie. I've—I've really enjoyed it."

"Me too," I admitted, suddenly feeling shy. "Um, I was kind of worried in the beginning."

"Why?"

I glanced down at my plate and poked at my salad. "I noticed you when you first came to Fairview. I kind of hoped— Well, but then I saw you hanging out with Jake and Fuzzy and all those guys. So I figured you were just like them."

"I'm not," he said softly.

I shrugged. "I know that now, I guess."

He must have sensed my hesitation, because he leaned forward and caught my eye. "Listen," he said. "Jake and Fuzzy and those guys don't matter. What matters is you and me. And I—I really like you, Andie." He took a breath, then went on.

"And I don't just mean because of the project. I don't just mean as a friend. I—"

"No!" I cried out in a strangled voice. I couldn't let him go on. Not until I knew whether he was sincere. Because if this was just another ploy to get me into bed, I knew it would probably break my heart—this time for good.

I took a deep breath. It was the moment of truth.

"Please," I said as calmly as I could. "Before you say anything else, I need to know. My reputation—I mean, I know you must have heard the stories. Or read some of the horrible things guys have written about me on the bathroom walls."

He sort of stammered in response to that. Obviously he knew exactly what I was talking about. I flushed, even though I'd known that by now he must have heard all the stories and then some. How could he not have?

I couldn't stand to look into his searching brown eyes anymore. Instead I stared down at my plate, though I wasn't seeing the food at all. I was looking into the past. "Once all those awful rumors started about what a nympho I was," I said bitterly, "that was that. No matter how much I denied the stories, no one believed me. And since I was new in town, it was really just me against everyone else."

He cleared his throat. "What happened?" he asked. "How did the rumors begin?"

There was a weird tone in his voice, but I

couldn't quite read it. That meant I had to decide on my own whether to go on. To trust him with the real story and take it from there. To put our friendship—or whatever—to the test, no matter what the consequences.

I just stared at him for a minute or two, trying to decide what to do. *I can't handle this,* I thought at first. *I can't go through it all again. Even if I tell him the truth, he might not believe me. He might think I'm just making excuses for blowing him off. That it's true what his friends say—that I'm a tease, a slut.*

Then again, it wasn't as though I could turn back time and take back what I'd already said. This conversation was going to take place sooner or later. I wouldn't be doing myself any favors by ignoring that fact.

I took a deep breath. And then, without really thinking about it anymore at all, I just started talking.

The whole story poured out of me. I hardly paused for breath as I told him everything—those first few afternoons hanging out with Fuzzy. The next few guys. The dawning realization of what was going on.

He didn't say much. Just sort of nodded and asked an occasional question. When I was finally finished—when the whole story was out, for better or for worse—he gazed at me for a moment, looking thoughtful and sort of sad.

Then he came around the table and perched in

the chair beside mine. "I'm so sorry," he said in a voice thick with emotion, reaching for my hand. "I have to admit, I've heard a lot of . . . stories . . . about you. And at first I wasn't sure what to think. But I should have known better. I should have asked for your side of the story before this. I'm sorry."

I just stared at him, hardly daring to believe what I was hearing. He believed me? He actually believed me!

It was all too much. After feeling completely alone for so long, it was as if I'd been rescued from a desert island. I'd found an ally—a friend. I collapsed against him.

"Thank you," I gasped in relief. "It just feels so good to tell someone about this. To feel like I finally have a—a friend."

His arms encircled me, making me feel safer and more relieved than ever. "I am your friend, Andie," he said, rubbing my shoulder gently. "Don't forget that. You can count on me."

Realizing that I was blubbering like a baby, I sat up and did my best to regain control. "Thanks," I said, glancing up at him. I wanted to say more, but I couldn't quite find the words just then. "I just— Thanks."

I'm not quite sure how it happened, but a few seconds later I was back in his arms. And we were kissing as though we might never stop.

This time I tried not to think. I just let myself float away on the feelings. It was amazing—better

than any kiss I'd ever experienced. Or even dreamed about.

After about a million years or so, A.J. pulled away. His eyes were soft and tender as they held mine. "That was nice."

"Really?" The word slipped out before I could stop it. I realized that I still hadn't totally let go of my fear. What if the kiss wasn't enough for A.J.? What if, even after all I'd told him, he still expected more? I didn't want to lose him. But I also didn't want to do anything I'd regret later.

Better safe than sorry, I decided. With an effort, I forced myself to pull away, out of his embrace. Settling back down onto my own chair, I cleared my throat. "Now you know my whole life story. What about you? Do you have any scandalous stories to tell?"

He didn't say anything for a minute or two, and I started to feel nervous. This was where he might grab me again, might get a little more forceful. Where I might be forced to fight him off, then kick him out of the house. Where we might never speak to each other again.

It was a relief when he finally spoke. "Actually," he said in a low, tentative voice I'd never heard him use before, "I do have a story. But it's not pretty."

"What?" I asked a little nervously. Was he going to confess to ruining some other girl's life the way Fuzzy and the others had ruined mine?

Or to rigging the egg project to be matched with me because he was looking to score?

His actual words were the last thing I would have guessed. "I wasn't always popular," he said, slowly and distinctly. "In fact, back in Chicago I was a major nerd."

I laughed briefly, certain that he must be kidding around. But I didn't get the joke. "What do you mean?"

He leaned back in his chair, though his eyes never left my face. "I mean I was a nerd. A geek. A dweeb. I played chess, belonged to all the academic clubs, and wore whatever happened to be clean and within arm's reach in the morning." He grimaced. "And actually, I wasn't even that strict about the clean part. Anyway, I was pretty happy for a long time. I mean, I was such a nerd that I wasn't really even aware that I *was* a nerd, if you know what I mean. I wore glasses and had a dorky haircut, but I was pretty tall, and I didn't trip over my own feet in gym class or anything. Besides, I was always willing to put in extra hours in my volunteer tutoring gig. So the cool kids pretty much left me alone."

I nodded, amazed at what he was telling me. How could it be true? I ran my eyes over him and saw the same thing I'd always seen: a cute, confident, popular guy. But I kept quiet, waiting for him to go on.

"All that changed last spring," he said quietly. "That's when I tutored a girl named Amber. She

was flunking algebra, and I helped her pull up her grade to a C." He paused, blinking a few times. "I also developed a huge crush on her."

"Oh," I said, suddenly realizing where this might be going. "Then what?"

"Then, after spending months worshiping the ground she walked on, I finally worked up the guts to ask her out." He grimaced. "Bad move. She practically laughed in my face. I can still remember what she said, practically word for word. 'Please,' she said, sort of looking around to see if anyone was watching us, 'I don't like to be rude, but can you stop talking to me before someone sees us together? It just doesn't work for my image if I'm seen all chatty with . . . with . . .' She kind of paused then—I guess she was struggling for the right word. Then she just sort of wrinkled her nose and went, 'With *you*.'"

I winced, imagining how hard it would be to hear something like that from someone I cared about. "Brutal," I commented softly.

A.J. shrugged. "Yeah," he said succinctly. "I took it kind of hard. I mean, even before that, I'd sort of vaguely noticed that her friends and mine didn't hang together much. But I guess I hadn't really stopped to think about it that much. I was too busy drooling over her." He sighed and sat up a little straighter. "But I guess I should thank her. It was just a couple of months later that Mom landed her new job and we decided to move. And because of what Amber said to me, and all the thinking I

did about it afterward, I decided to change my life." He shrugged again. "And so I did."

"Wow." I didn't know what else to say. I remained silent for a moment, mulling over what he'd just told me. It was hard to believe he'd been as big a geek as he claimed. Still, it explained the sweet, sensitive side of him. It also explained why he'd never quite seemed to match with Jake and the others. I'd thought that was wishful thinking, but now that didn't seem to be the case. A.J. had only sought out the jock crowd because he'd wanted to be popular—not because he actually liked them.

But when I tried to point that out, he protested, saying that he actually liked his new pals. "They're fun to be around," he said. "And they're really good guys once you get to know them. Sometimes they just don't think about, you know, other people."

"Like me." I knew I sounded kind of bitter, but I couldn't help it. Still, I didn't want to make him feel bad, especially after he'd just poured out his heart to me. "Don't worry," I told him, grabbing his hand and squeezing it. "I'm not mad about who your new friends are. It doesn't matter. Not anymore, now that I know I can trust you."

I guess the whole idea of trusting someone again, after so long standing on my own, sort of overwhelmed me a little. Because before I knew what I was doing, I was kissing him again.

And this time neither of us pulled away for a long, long time.

Six

I HAD TO work at the library all day on Sunday, so I didn't get a chance to see A.J. But I was thinking about him the whole time I was shelving, checking out books, and tracking down the reference materials Courtney needed for her report.

When Monday morning arrived, for the first time in ages I was actually eager to get to school. I found A.J. at his locker before homeroom and we spent a few minutes hanging out, just sort of talking about everything and nothing.

The rest of the day went pretty well. In psych class Ms. Church gave us some time at the end of class to work on our reports. Courtney was so thrilled with the books I'd found that she kept glancing over at me and waving happily. And right after class Lauren stopped me in the hall to thank me for the costume books, which I'd left for her at her locker.

Wow, I thought as Lauren and I parted ways, noticing a few of the other kids in the hall around us shooting me curious—but not hostile—glances. *If this keeps up, I may actually start eating lunch in the cafeteria again. I may actually wake up one day and find myself . . . popular!*

I couldn't help laughing at that thought. Still, I also couldn't help crossing my fingers and hoping that it might be true.

All in all, I was feeling pretty lighthearted by the time the final bell rang. A.J. and I had talked about getting together after dinner that evening—not for the project this time, but just because we wanted to be together. I shivered in anticipation just thinking about kissing him again.

But first I had to get through my shift at the library. I grabbed the books I needed for that night's homework out of my locker and headed for the back door, which led out past the gym. It was the way I always left, partly to avoid as many people as possible, and partly because it was a shortcut when I was headed to the university.

On my way I passed Courtney and Marissa, who were leaning against the wall outside the girls' locker room. Even though Courtney and Lauren were being nice to me now, I definitely wasn't too comfortable around Marissa. But for once I decided not to let her snotty attitude stop me. "Hi, guys. How's it going?"

Courtney nodded stiffly at me but didn't respond. She glanced at Marissa. "I've got to go," she

murmured. "I want to get changed and start warming up before the other girls get here. My knees feel a little whacked today."

Without another word or even a glance at me, she hurried through the locker room door. I stared after her, perplexed. "What's with her?" I asked, almost forgetting whom I was talking to.

Marissa barked out a short laugh. "I guess she didn't want to stick around and hear all the down-and-dirty details about your weekend."

I gasped, not quite understanding, but knowing that this couldn't be good. "What do you mean?"

Marissa shrugged lazily. "You can cut the innocent act. I already heard all about your night with Andy." She shook her head. "And right after Courtney spent all weekend trying to defend your honor. Saying you weren't the kind of girl who would hit the rug with all those guys."

My jaw dropped. If this was déjà vu, it was the worst case I'd ever had. "A.J. and I kissed, but that was it!" I protested angrily. "Why are you always lying about me?"

"Me? Ha! You should ask your precious *A.J.*"—Marissa put a little extra emphasis on the nickname, which had slipped out without my realizing it—"what he has been saying about you. He told the guys you two slept together on Saturday night. Again."

I felt like I'd been slapped. "A.J. wouldn't say that."

Marissa snorted and rolled her eyes, tossing her long auburn hair. "Look, princess. We're all getting

really tired of this victim act you keep putting on." She stood up and took a step toward the locker room door as several other girls approached, chatting and laughing with each other. "I know *I'm* way tired of hearing it. 'Poor little me, I haven't done anything.'" She curled her lip in disgust. "Just be honest already. You're a slut."

I gasped for air, unable to respond or even to think. Marissa watched me for a moment, like a scientist watching a bug squirm after it's been pinned to a card. Then she turned and followed the other girls into the locker room.

I'm not sure how I made it to the library after that. I certainly wasn't aware of where I was or what I was doing for the next hour or so. All I could think about was what Marissa had told me. And how A.J. had betrayed me.

I trusted him, I thought over and over again. *I trusted him, and this is what happens.*

It was so painful that I couldn't even cry. All I could do was try to survive. To keep breathing, and not spontaneously self-destruct out of the sheer humiliation and pain of it all.

I don't know how long I'd been at the library when A.J. walked in. For a second I couldn't quite believe that he was actually there. What did he want?

He started babbling about wanting to ask me something, not even seeming to notice that anything was wrong. Finally I couldn't take it anymore. Stomping off to the back room, I grabbed Eggbert

out of his carrying case. Then I returned and started telling A.J. exactly what I thought of him and what he'd done.

He denied it at first. But eventually he realized that I was on to him. He claimed he'd never said anything to the guys—that they'd just made some assumptions, and he hadn't quite managed to correct them. As if there were a difference. Either way, I was toast.

When I was so fed up that I was ready to explode, I did the only thing I could think of to express how totally happy I would be if I never set eyes on Andrew Jackson Parker again. I cracked Eggbert open, right over his daddy's cool new haircut.

That made me feel a little better. At least for long enough for me to escape to the staff room.

That's when I finally started to cry. So hard that I was afraid I might never be able to stop.

Seven

A.J. CALLED MY house about a million times that night. He even came by once in person. But I refused to see him or talk to him. I let the machine pick up every time he called, and when he stopped by and rang the doorbell, I watched through a crack in my bedroom curtain until he walked away.

The next day I thought about staying home and pretending I had the flu. But I knew there wasn't much point. I would have to go back to Fairview High someday, like it or not. I might as well get it over with.

Still, I guess something showed on my face, because when I came downstairs to breakfast, Mom took one look at me and dropped the cereal box she was holding. Hurrying over, she took me in her arms. "Andie, love, what's the matter?"

I hesitated. I'd never told her about my experiences at Fairview because I hadn't wanted her to

worry about me. I still didn't. But I couldn't go on alone anymore. Not after everything that had happened.

"Mom," I said, my voice cracking, "there's so much you don't know. So much I never told you. . . ."

"Tell me now."

I nodded, took a deep breath, and told her everything.

Okay, Fairview High, I thought as I stepped through the school's front doors a little while later. *Take your best shot. I'm ready.*

The halls were quiet. Thanks to my breakfast confession, I was late to first period, but Mom had written me a note. In fact, she'd offered to let me stay home from school for a day or two if I chose, and it was tempting. But once again I'd decided it was better to face the music right away rather than put it off.

After stopping in the school office for a tardy slip, I headed to my first class. Courtney was in the class, sitting right in the front row, but I kept my eyes on the teacher as I walked in and handed her my excuse. If I looked at Courtney and she turned away in disgust, I was afraid I might break down in front of everyone.

When the class ended I gathered up my books and hurried out of the room as quickly as possible. To my surprise, Courtney caught up to me in the hall.

"Andie," she said, putting a hand on my arm. "Can I walk with you?"

I hesitated, wondering what new punishment was in store for me. Then I shrugged. "Sure."

She fell into step beside me as I headed toward second period. "I just wanted to thank you again for those books," she said in her soft, musical voice. "They're really helping Kyle and me a lot with our report."

"No big," I replied. I expected her to move on, duty done, but instead she continued to walk with me.

After a moment of silence, she spoke up again. "Also, I wanted to say that I'm, like, really sorry." She swallowed hard. "Um, I know I was rude yesterday. You know, after school. It was because of what Kyle told me about . . . you know. I was, like, totally furious. I thought you'd been lying to me about all that."

I waited for her to get to the point. "Yes?"

"Anyway, I should have known better." She shrugged. "Kyle and his big mouth! It wasn't until last night while we were hanging out that I figured it out. Andy didn't actually tell him that you two hooked up on Saturday night. Kyle and Jake and the rest of them just sort of assumed it."

She shot me a glance, obviously wondering how I was taking all this. Honestly, I wasn't sure how to respond. I already knew what she was telling me. What difference did it make? Everyone still thought I was the school skank.

"Okay, well, I just wanted you to know I'm sorry," she went on at last. "I should have trusted you. You've been a nice friend to me lately, and I

was, like, totally too quick to judge. I'm sorry. Can you ever forgive me?"

I had to smile at the earnest look on her face. "Sure," I said. "Why not?"

Courtney looked relieved. We parted ways soon after that to go to our separate classes, and I was left thinking about what she'd said. Yes, I could forgive her. She'd made a mistake and owned up to it.

Besides, I thought as I hurried down the hall, still avoiding eye contact with everyone I passed, *she's not the one who really betrayed me.*

As much as I wished second period would end, I dreaded the arrival of third period even more: psych class, when I would have to face A.J.

All too soon it was time. I hovered in the hall around the corner from the classroom, wanting to duck inside at the last possible moment. Maybe that way I wouldn't have to look at him at all until after class.

My little plan worked. I scooted into the room just steps ahead of Ms. Church. I sensed rather than saw A.J. staring at me from his seat beside Jake. But I wasn't about to give him the satisfaction of looking at him and giving him any clue as to how I was feeling.

Ms. Church started class, talking about the project and everything we were supposed to have learned. But I wasn't really listening. Instead I was fuming about what A.J. had reduced me to. Now I had to skulk around school, trying to avoid him so

I wouldn't get my feelings hurt anymore. Why should I bother? What more could he and his friends do to me?

Right then and there, I decided that it was time to make a change. I wasn't going to hide behind my reputation any longer. I wasn't going to be a coward. From now on, I was going to stick up for myself more and worry less about what other people thought of me. Maybe Courtney and Lauren would still want to be my friends. Maybe not. Either way, people were about to meet a new, improved Andie Foster.

I sat up a little straighter in my chair. Wendell Owen glanced at me curiously, and I glared at him. He shrugged and returned his attention to Ms. Church, making me feel a little guilty. Wendell had never done anything to me.

Still, I stiffened my backbone and kept on sitting straight and tall. I also started to pay attention to what Ms. Church was saying. "I know you've all learned a lot during the past week," the teacher said, clasping her hands behind her back and pacing back and forth across the front of the classroom. Then she stopped and shot us a mischievous smile. "Now, I have to admit I'm going to be a bit sexist here today. I'm going to ask the husbands to be the ones to deliver your oral reports about what you've learned from this experience."

A loud collective male groan rang out, followed by female cheers. There were some things everyone could agree on, no matter what social group

they belonged to—like not wanting to give oral reports.

Ms. Church held up her hand for attention. "There's a reason for that. I believe the guys probably learned more about marriage and fatherhood than they'd bargained for."

"I definitely got a lot more than I bargained for," Jake groused loudly.

Everyone laughed—even me, a little. I hadn't been paying much attention to Jake's progress on the project, but even I was aware of the way he'd gradually lost interest in his "wife," Veronica, in favor of his ex-girlfriend, Marissa. From the way both of them were glaring at him at that moment, I guessed that his juggling act hadn't been as successful as he might have hoped.

As the laughter died down, A.J. raised his hand. "Ms. Church?" he said, his voice quavering slightly. "I'd like to give my report first, if that's all right."

Ms. Church shrugged, looking surprised. "Of course it's all right, Mr. Parker," she said. "I thought I'd have to bribe some poor sucker to go first."

Most of the class chuckled at that, but A.J.'s face remained serious as he picked up our project notebook and walked to the front of the room. I wasn't feeling much like laughing right at the moment either.

What's he up to now? I wondered, my stomach flip-flopping nervously. Despite my anger, I couldn't help noticing that A.J. looked awfully cute

standing up there in front of the blackboard. His dark eyes were serious as he glanced down at our notebook without opening it.

Then he cleared his throat and looked around the room, his gaze lingering only slightly longer on me than on anyone else. For a second our eyes locked, but I looked away.

That's when A.J. started to speak. "For me, this project turned out to be a lot different from what I'd expected," he began. "When I took on the pretend role of husband and father, I learned a lot about what it means to be a grown-up. The obvious things I'm talking about are the same things everyone here probably learned—accepting responsibility for a baby's life, making money, learning to compromise, figuring out what it means to make a home, and of course sharing in the child care responsibilities."

He held up our journal. "All of that is in the report Andie Foster and I wrote. It was the official part of the assignment." He set the notebook on Ms. Church's desk and wiped his hands on his jeans, looking nervous. "But more than that, I learned that I had a lot of growing up to do. When I came to Fairview High a couple of weeks ago, I was only concerned with myself and creating a good impression. Being cool was all that mattered to me because it meant I was going to be a very different kind of person." He paused and took a deep breath, and I noticed that his hands were shaking a little. "That's because back

at my old school in Chicago, I was a major nerd."

Jake hooted loudly with laughter. "Yeah, right," he called out. "Good one, man!"

A.J. held up his hands as the rest of the class started murmuring. Even Wendell was shaking his head in confusion. "No, really," A.J. protested. "I was a chess-loving, *Star Trek*–obsessed dweeb. I was smart and I liked being smart. I wore the wrong kind of clothes. I hung out with the wrong kind of kids. And I definitely didn't have a girlfriend."

I frowned, trying to figure out why he was doing this. Why would he sabotage his status now? It didn't make sense.

"Anyway," A.J. went on, "when I learned I'd be moving and coming to a new school, I decided to reinvent myself. And it worked. I found myself hanging out with the cool crowd. And even—" He hesitated again, glancing at me. "I even found myself falling in love with a cool girl. My 'wife,' Andie Foster."

I felt my face turning beet red. My spine stayed straight, but inside I felt like sinking into the floor. Why was he doing this to me? Hadn't he humiliated me enough already?

And he wasn't finished. "Once I became Andie's husband," he said, "I discovered that I was more popular than ever. It didn't take long to figure out why. Everyone said she was easy, so they all just assumed that we were fooling around."

The room was so quiet that you could have heard a flea sneeze. Ms. Church opened her

mouth, and for a moment I thought she was going to stop A.J.'s little speech then and there. But she closed her mouth again without making a sound and just leaned back against her desk, listening along with everyone else.

"Soon guys I barely knew were slapping me on the back and calling me a stud," A.J. said. "At first it was great, and I figured nobody would get hurt as long as I never mentioned it to Andie. But I was wrong. Somebody did get hurt. And it was all my fault."

Jake snorted loudly. "What's up here?" he called out, sounding angry. "This is total crap. Plus it has nothing to do with the assignment."

Ms. Church cut him off with an upraised hand. "I agree, Mr. Wilkins, that Mr. Parker's report isn't quite what I expected. But it sounds like what Andy has learned this week has everything to do with the essence of egg week. Please continue, Andy."

A.J. nodded his thanks. "The point is, I listened to gossip and even added to it, sort of, just because I was afraid to stand up and tell the truth. But I'm not afraid anymore. I figured out there really are more important things than being popular. And I hope you'll all believe me when I tell you that none of the stuff you've heard about Andie is true. A couple of guys just got their feelings hurt and then started getting competitive with each other. That's when they made up all those stories about Andie."

He paused and blinked at Jake, Fuzzy, and Kyle,

then continued, "And I'm really sorry if you don't think I'm cool enough to be your friend anymore. But I refuse to be a coward and a liar any longer." Then he turned his gaze on me. "Andie?" he said softly. "How about it? Will you give me a second chance?"

The whole class turned to stare at me as well, waiting for my reaction. I just sat there for a second, trying to ride it out. But then I lost it. Bursting into tears, I stood up and ran blindly out of the room.

Eight

I WAS SITTING at the desk in the media library, almost all cried out, when the door opened and A.J. poked his head in. "There you are!" he exclaimed, sounding relieved.

I glared at him. "What do you want now?" I snapped.

He looked a bit startled. "Um, Ms. Church said I could come after you." His voice sounded breathless and his eyes were overly bright. "She thought we might have some things to say to each other, I guess."

"I have nothing to say to you." I turned my back to him, staring out the window above the desk. The sky was steel gray, and a few flakes of snow were spiraling toward the earth. I suddenly remembered hearing somewhere that no two snowflakes were alike. Each one of the millions and billions that fell to earth was unique, different from all its

brothers and sisters. It was a lonely thought.

A.J. cleared his throat. "But didn't you hear what I said back there?" He sounded wounded. "I did what you wanted. I told everyone the truth."

I was so amazed at his words that I turned around to face him again, staring at him in disbelief. "What on earth made you think that was what I wanted?" I demanded. "When did I ever suggest that I wanted to be publicly humiliated yet again?"

"Humil— But I told them you weren't like they thought!" he protested. "I defended you!"

"Gee, thanks," I replied, my voice oozing sarcasm. "And when your jock buddies start giving you a hard time in the lunchroom today, what are you going to say then? That it was all a big joke? Or worse yet, a ploy to get me to forgive you—so I'd keep sharing the goodies all night, every night?"

"No way." His voice was firm. "This time I'm not backing down. I'm going to tell them all the truth, as many times as it takes to make them believe it."

"Yeah, right." I rolled my eyes. "I know how important being popular is to you. You'll back down as soon as Jake looks at you cross-eyed."

"You're wrong," he said fiercely, taking another step into the small room. "I'm not making that mistake again. I admit it, I liked being popular. But I decided something yesterday. The price just wasn't worth it."

I hesitated, looking at him carefully. Did he

actually mean what he was saying? Had he really flushed his popularity down the toilet . . . for me?

Sensing something in my expression, he moved closer and took hold of my hand. I stared down at his long, strong fingers and thought how good my hand felt in his. "Come to the Valentine's dance with me," he said in a husky voice. "Please?"

"What?" I yanked my hand away from his, not believing his nerve. Not believing I'd been on the verge of forgiving him. "How dare you?"

"I want to make it up to you."

"And you think if I get to go to a dance with you, that will be enough? A date with you will make up for all the humiliation and hurt I've suffered?" My voice was getting louder and louder, but I didn't care. He'd embarrassed me in front of the world. The least I could do was return the favor.

"Come on, Andie," he pleaded. "You've got to give me a second chance. I—I don't know what I'll do otherwise."

I was about to snap out a quick, mean response. But then I saw something glinting in the corner of one brown eye. "Are you crying?" I asked in amazement. Various guys had tried various things to win me over in the past, but none of them had resorted to tears.

"No, of course not." A.J. swiped at his face. He gulped. "Well, okay, so maybe I am. Because I can't imagine going on at this school without you to talk to and laugh with and . . . and just be with. Andie, I—" He gulped. "Andie Foster, I love you."

I gasped, my head swimming. "What did you say?"

"I love you." This time the words were stronger. He stepped forward again, and this time I didn't pull my hand away. Instead I gazed up at him in wonder. How could three little words sweep away all the pain of the past twenty-four hours? How could they make up for months of misery and resentment?

And yet somehow, magically, they did.

Oh, don't get me wrong. A.J. and I had a whole lot of talks after that. Serious talks. And it was quite a while before I could really forget about what had happened and open up completely again.

But it was a start. And standing there in the tiny media room, with snowflakes swirling down faster and faster outside, he leaned down to kiss me again, his lips tender but anxious.

And again, I didn't pull away.

Nine

THE VALENTINE'S DAY dance was just as amazing as Courtney had promised me it would be. The band was smoking, the decorating committee had plastered hundreds of red hearts over every inch of the gym, and even the snacks and punch were delicious. Amazing, considering that they came from the same cafeteria that tortured us with cold Salisbury steak, gray pea mush, and other disgusting delicacies every day.

Oh, yes. I was eating in the cafeteria now. For the first few days A.J. and I had sat at a table by ourselves. Then, one by one, his friends had started wandering over to join us partway through the period. Courtney and Lauren were first, followed by Jake and Kyle and Fuzzy. Eventually even Marissa had become a regular. Before I knew it, we were all hanging out together—not only at lunch, but between classes and after school.

Now, standing by the punch bowl in the new red velvet sheath dress I'd bought out of my last library paycheck, I tried to remember the last time I'd been this happy. Glancing at A.J., who was chatting with Wendell Owen nearby, I decided that I'd never been so happy. Because as horrible as most of that year had been, I was glad it had happened. If I'd never moved to Fairview, I might never have met A.J.

As if reading my mind, he said good-bye to Wendell and came over to slip his arm around me. "Having fun?" he murmured, leaning over to make himself heard over the pounding music.

I nodded and smiled up at him. "I'm having a blast," I replied. "Want to dance? I like this song."

"Sure."

We moved out onto the dance floor and soon found ourselves boogying next to Jake and Marissa. They'd patched up their differences after the egg project ended, and now they couldn't seem to stop gazing at each other and kissing every chance they got. It was driving all the teachers crazy, but I thought it was cute.

Amazing, I thought as Marissa glanced over at me, waved, and smiled. A couple of weeks earlier I'd thought I would never be able to forgive what Jake, Marissa, and their friends had put me through. But to my amazement, after we started eating lunch together, each of them had made a point of coming up to me privately and apologizing for his or her part in the whole mess. Even Fuzzy

had sort of mumbled something resembling an apology one day on our way out of the cafeteria. I realized I appreciated his words even more than the others', because I knew how hard they were for him to say.

"Is something wrong?" A.J. asked, pulling me closer. "You look kind of serious."

"No, nothing's wrong." I smiled at him. "I was just thinking about our friends. And how important second chances can be."

A.J. nodded. "That's for sure," he agreed, wrapping his arms around me and swaying slowly back and forth, even though the band was playing a fast song. "I'll never stop being grateful that you gave me a second chance, even though I probably didn't deserve one."

I tipped my head up until our lips were only an inch apart. "Oh, you deserved it all right," I murmured. "This was worth all the trouble. Definitely."

"Really?" He grinned mischievously, leaning even closer until our lips were almost grazing. "Does that mean if I play my cards right, I might get lucky?"

"No," I answered as our breath mingled. "But you might get a kiss."

"Oh, really?" His lips skimmed the corner of my mouth. "I think I could live with that."

We kissed for an endless moment, hardly aware of the dancers surrounding us. Finally I pulled away and smiled at him. "Happy Valentine's Day," I said.

"Same to you," A.J. replied huskily. He stroked my cheek with one hand. "I love you."

I closed my eyes, enjoying the gentle caress of his fingers. When I opened them again, he was still gazing at me with a world of emotion in his deep brown eyes.

I sighed happily as we began to sway again to our own private music. "I love you too, Andrew Jackson Parker."

WIN A UNIONBAY WARDROBE
OFFICIAL RULES & REGULATIONS

I. HOW TO ENTER

NO PURCHASE NECESSARY. Enter by printing your name, address, phone number, date of birth, and description (500 words or less) of your first love, and mail to: UNIONBAY & LOVE STORIES WARDROBE CONTEST, Random House Children's Marketing Department, 1540 Broadway, 20th Floor, New York, NY 10036. Entries must be received by Random House no later than March 1, 2000. LIMIT ONE ENTRY PER PERSON. Random House will not be able to return your submission, so please keep a copy for your records.

II. ELIGIBILITY

Contest is open to residents of the United States, excluding the state of Arizona, who are between the ages of 14 and 21 as of January 1, 2000. All federal, state, and local regulations apply. Void wherever prohibited or restricted by law. Employees of Random House, Inc., UNIONBAY, their parent, subsidiaries and affiliates, and their immediate families, and persons living in their household are not eligible to enter this contest. Random House is not responsible for lost, stolen, illegible, incomplete, postage due or misdirected entries.

III. PRIZE

One winner will win a wardrobe of UNIONBAY clothing (approximate retail value $500.00 US).

IV. WINNER

Entries will be judged by Random House Children's Marketing Department Staff on the basis of originality, style, and creativity. One winner will be chosen on or about March 15, 2000 from all eligible entries received within the entry deadline by the Random House Children's Marketing Department. Only the winner will be notified. The prize will be awarded in the name of the winner or the winner's parent or legal guardian, if winner is under age 18. Winner will be notified by mail on or about March 30, 2000. Taxes, if any, are the winner's sole responsibility. Winner (or the winner's parent or legal guardian, if winner is under age 18) will be required to execute and return within 14 days of notification, affidavits of eligibility and release. A noncompliance within that time period or the return of any notification as undeliverable will result in disqualification and the selection of an alternate winner. In the event of any other noncompliance with rules and conditions, prize may be awarded to an alternate winner.

V. RESERVATIONS

By entering the contest you consent to the use of your name, likeness, and biographical data for publicity and promotional purposes on behalf of Random House and UNIONBAY with no additional compensation or further permission (except where prohibited by law). Other entry names will NOT be used for subsequent mail solicitation. For the names of the winners, available after March 30, 2000, please send a stamped, self-addressed envelope to: Random House Children's Marketing Department, UNIONBAY Wardrobe Winners, 1540 Broadway, 20th Floor, New York, NY 10036.

WIN A UNIONBAY WARDROBE!

Here's one story we know you'll love. Score $500 worth of new duds from UnBeatably hip clothiers UNIONBAY. All you have to do to enter is tell us about *your* first love.

(See next page for contest rules and regulations.)

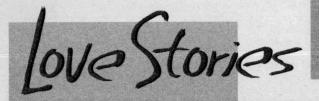

Love Stories

...You'll always remember your first love.

Super Editions